COLIN EVANS

AuthorHouse™ UK
1663 Liberty Drive
Bloomington, IN 47403 USA
www.authorhouse.co.uk
Phone: 0800.197.4150

© 2014 Colin Evans. All rights reserved.

No part of this book may be reproduced, stored in a retrieval system, or transmitted by any means without the written permission of the author.

Published by AuthorHouse   12/01/2014

ISBN: 978-1-4969-9721-0 (sc)
ISBN: 978-1-4969-9722-7 (e)

Any people depicted in stock imagery provided by Thinkstock are models, and such images are being used for illustrative purposes only.
Certain stock imagery © Thinkstock.

This book is printed on acid-free paper.

Because of the dynamic nature of the Internet, any web addresses or links contained in this book may have changed since publication and may no longer be valid. The views expressed in this work are solely those of the author and do not necessarily reflect the views of the publisher, and the publisher hereby disclaims any responsibility for them.

So mankind believe they are the most intelligent and the most important animals living on this planet.

Now I expect I have upset a few of you good people already simply by calling our species animals. However, of course, it is what we are.

Nevertheless, some people believe that because of our so-called "superior intelligence" we are above all the other life forms that share with us this island in space, which we all call home.

Okay then, so if this is correct why are we the only animal on this planet that's stupid enough to quite happily destroy everything that's here solely for our own gain? Now there's something to ponder over don't you think?

Oops, sorry about that, of course we don't need to think, about anything do we. Because we are, after all the "superior beings" and we own this planet and are free to do whatever we please with it. And we already know all the answers to everything because we don't miss a thing, silly me. Therefore, why in our infinite wisdom are we polluting and destroying everything that life needs to exist on this planet, and knowingly and quite willingly doing so, all in the name of profit.

Or to put it another way we are destroying the planet, ourselves, and everything else that's here for money.

Not a good strategy really is it. Now before you go off on one and start labelling me as whatever, let me just say I am not a tree hugger. I don't answer to the name swampy nor am I a member of Greenpeace, the WWF, Friends of the Earth or the WDC; although I must admit, I have nothing but the utmost respect for these people and all their accomplishments.

Now I don't belong to any form of Eco warriors for you. I am not a member of the BNP, Al qaeda, or a member of the telly tubby fan club, and I don't have a

Blue peter badge either. I am just a person in the street with something to say about what we are doing to this planet and the amazing creatures that also live here.

Let's compare ourselves to all the other life forms that share this planet with us, now if you think about it every other life form on this planet finds its own natural equilibrium. And appear to be in balance with the natural world and the surroundings they have chosen to live in, and they build their homes out of natural things, such as mud, twigs grass, feathers, fur, and moss for their nests and burrows, all of which is biodegradable. Therefore, it eventually decomposes and goes back into the land where it came from when it's finished with. And these creatures have evolved and adjusted over time to live on this world and appear to be in harmony with nature and they seem quite happy to abide by her rules.

Now let me give you a little history lesson if I may, sixty five million years ago a ten kilometre Asteroid collided with this planet with a force equivalent to ninety-six teratons of TNT, apparently it's what killed off the dinosaurs it also wiped out at least half of all known life on this planet. Except of course for the surviving creatures, (obviously) some of which I have mentioned in this book. For example the saltwater crocodile, that has been on this planet practically unchanged for two hundred million years.

Then there are the green turtles that I mention later on that have been here for two hundred and twenty million years. The great white shark (which is also now under threat) has been here for four hundred million years.

However, the majority of all shellfish have survived on this planet practically unchanged for an incredible four hundred and ninety million years.

And every single one of these creatures has become perfectly adapted for their way of life, for example, the Nile crocodile's heart has evolved so it can redirect blood to certain vital parts of its body, which allows it to stay submerged for over an hour at a time on a single breath.

Then of course, you have us, the Homo sapiens. (Intelligent man) who have only been here for an estimated two hundred thousand years, or we can look at it this way. The planet earth is 4.6 billion years old now if you scale that down to 46 years, then humans have only been here for four hours, and the industrial revolution started just one minute ago, and in that single minute we have destroyed over half the world's rainforest. Yet we have now put all of these "survivors" in danger once more, through our own greed and our stupidity.

Because humanity who for some reason are vain enough too immediately, class themselves as the "superior beings" on this planet, through the fact that they are intelligent enough to build a completely artificial world to live in using artificial and unnatural things to do so.

For example reinforced concrete, tarmac, artificial lighting, cars, Lorries, plastic, and the list just goes on and on. However, humanity needs to realise that by building this artificial world they are also destroying the real world, along with everything they need for their very survival, including the planet we all live on which I wouldn't have thought was the most intelligent thing to do somehow. Furthermore, humanity have continually made changes to this world so that it suits their requirements regardless of the consequences, and appear to think that everything on this planet including all the other life forms and even the planet itself are here solely for humanity's use, they even make whatever god they worship in their own image.

We even breed animals to look a certain way, for example, the English bulldog that have become so inbred over the years that they now suffer from all sorts of ailments such as respiratory problems, and they also have great difficulty in giving birth to their pups because of the size of their heads. However, none of that matters in the slightest, simply because some people think they "look nice."

They do the same sort of thing to cats so they have a "nice flat face" that makes them look really cute, it's just a shame the cat can't breathe properly. However, that's just a minor detail because once again some people think they look nice. Humanity just can't help themselves, and feel they have to improve (interfere) along with a constant desire to control and change everything so it suits their needs and requirements.

None of which helps the environment, the other life forms, or the planet In fact, it's the complete opposite and is now a scientifically proven fact to be one of if not the, main cause of our problems, especially deforestation and the burning of fossil fuels along with the greenhouse gases created as a result. We already know the end of all fossil fuels is rapidly approaching, yet many people still refuse to accept it as a proven fact and some believe it to be "made up" just to scare people, which to me seems to be a lot of work to go through for a practical joke.

However just like any animal that doesn't have any natural predators (except of course ourselves) mankind has just spiralled out of control, so mankind have now become too big for the planet (and also too big for their boots) because they truly believe they are invincible.

Now spindle cells, which all humans have in their D.N.A, are responsible for recognition, speech, memory, and so on therefore, these spindle cells play a very important part in intelligence. Well recently, scientists have proven how whales, dolphins, the great apes, and elephants possess three times the amount of these spindle cells in their D.N.A compared to humanity. So are we really the most intelligent animal on this planet?

Experts in their relative fields have written several lengthy papers on the subject the following is a summary of one of these papers. Now I have written this book in layman terms, simply because like many readers it's what I am, and I will also admit to sometimes finding a lot of the professional's writing hard to understand, and quite often boring (no offence meant) so I will apologize in advance because some of the following does get a bit technical. Humanity believes they deserve their "superior status" over the other animals because of these scientific truths, which are. Only humans are self-aware and feel empathy, we are unique in our abilities to use language and tools, we are the only animals that can recognize themselves in a mirror, and capable of realising the passing of time. However, advances in cognitive ethology (the scientific study of animal intelligence, emotions, behaviour, and social life) have now disproved these "truths" by showing that many other creatures can also display a complex range of emotions. Along with highly evolved communication skills, the ability to show compassion for others, and intelligence that rivals, or even surpasses our own so now, these ground breaking studies forces humanity to ask some very uncomfortable questions about our place in this world. So many leading experts are now calling for a major rethink on the way we treat the other animals that share this world with us.

And among the findings, they discovered that, fish do feel pain, and acidic water makes them nervous. Chickens are not only very intelligent creatures they can also feel each other's pain and show physiological signs of concern and distress over the suffering of their young.

Research suggests that rats are also compassionate, communicative, and highly intelligent creatures. Scientists also discovered that rats would prefer to free other rats from their cages rather than helping themselves to food, and no one had taught the rats how to open the cages before they done the experiment.

So briefly, they would put helping their friends as their top priority before feeding themselves, because it could have quite easily eaten all the food but chose not to.

Older studies from the 1950s and 60s discovered that both rats and rhesus monkeys would refuse to pull a lever that released food if it also resulted in an electric shock befalling another member of its group, and one monkey went completely without food for a total of twelve days rather than hurt one of its group.

Another researcher who was attempting to free two baby mice that were trapped in a sink noticed that the stronger of the two showed concern for his exhausted friend, he also carried food to his friend until he was strong enough to move.

Furthermore, some of the most heart-warming tales of expressive love and empathy come from our closest relatives, which are of course the great apes, and here's one of them that some of you might remember.

Binti jua, a female gorilla at Brookfield Zoo in Illinois, had her fifteen minutes of fame in 1996 when she went to help a three-year-old boy who had been sitting on the wall of the gorilla enclosure and slipped, he fell five metres onto the concrete floor below. Binti Jua gently lifted the unconscious boy and cradled him in her arms, growling warnings at the other gorillas that attempted to get close to the child, then while her own infant clung to her back she gently carried the boy to the Zoo staff who was waiting for her at the enclosures gates.

Then there is the story of a captive Bonobo chimpanzee named Kuni that lives in the United Kingdom, who one day came across a starling that had been stunned by flying into something. Therefore, Kuni picked the starling up with one hand, and climbed to the top of the highest tree in her enclosure, she then wrapped her legs around the trees trunk so she had both hands free to hold the bird. She then very carefully opened its wings as far as they would go and she threw the bird as hard as she could towards the boundary wall of her enclosure; however, the starling didn't wake up and landed on the bank of the enclosures moat.

Now although her rescue attempt wasn't successful, Kuni was most certainly acting out of good intentions, and she attempted to make amends by guarding the unconscious and vulnerable bird from a curious juvenile for quite some time.

Therefore, it's now being argued that humanity does not have complete monopoly on moral behaviour. And there are an incredible amount of stories to prove it, for example, a teenage female elephant who was nursing an injured leg was knocked over by a teenage male, and an older female watches it happen and quickly chases the young male away, she then returns to the young female and massages her injured leg with her trunk.

Then there were the eleven elephants that rescued a group of captured antelope in Kwazula-Natal. The Matriarch elephant undone every latch on the gates of the enclosure with her trunk and allowed the gates to swing open so the antelope could escape.

A male Diana monkey who had learned to insert a token into a slot to get food helps a female who just couldn't seem to get the hang of it, so he puts the token in for her and lets her eat the food.

And a female fruit bat who helps an unrelated female to give birth by showing her how to hang in the proper way. Or the cat named Libby who helps her friend Cashew who is an elderly deaf and blind dog by leading it away from obstacles and towards its food.

There is a group of chimpanzees living in the Arnhelm Zoo in the Netherlands, where individuals will punish other members of its group if they are late for a meal, because no one's allowed to start eating until everybody is present. Also recently, there was the story of an abandoned Pit-bull puppy named Rosie, which was born deaf. So her owners decided not to keep her and gave her to a rescue centre where it took three months for Rosie to learn how to respond to commands that were given to her with the use of sign language; eventually a deaf woman who now intends to carry on training Rosie using sign language adopted her.

Then you have the woman who claims someone had kidnapped her when she was five years old, and how her captor had then abandoned her in the jungle. She also claims to have been cared for and brought up by a group of Capuchin monkeys, and stated she had lived with these monkeys for at least five years before some people who were walking through the forest discovered her. And had taken her to a city where they had sold her as a slave until she managed to escape.

And how at the age of sixty-two, her daughter finally talked her into writing a book about it all, and many people, including the press instantly started calling her a liar, and a fraud. So she eventually (and at her own cost) agreed to take a trip back to the forest where she claims to have lived, she also went to the city where she had been sold as a slave. She managed to find the house where she had been held captive, and spoke to the neighbour who remembered the woman who had bought her; she also remembered seeing a little girl there.

The sixty-two year old woman also agreed to undergo a wide variety of tests, including one similar to a lie detector, all of which she passed with flying colours, therefore, it has now been scientifically proven that her story is true. There are quite a few similar stories, such as the Indian boy who was discovered living with wolves in 1954. Or the story of a young Russian boy who was found living with dogs in the 1980's.

So do these examples show that animals display moral behaviour, that they can be compassionate, altruistic, and fair? A great deal of people believe it does (and I agree with them) because animals not only have a sense of justice, a sense of empathy, along with forgiveness, trust, reciprocity, and a great deal more. Furthermore, these good emotions can be shared by the most unlikely of friends. Including predators and prey, such as a cat and a bird, a lioness and a baby Oryx, a cheetah and a retriever and even a tortoise and a goose, cats have been known to adopt abandoned chicks and even baby hedgehogs, and that's just a few of many examples.

One recent case involved a disabled dolphin that had been "adopted" by a family of sperm whales so it appears that compassion knows no boundaries.

Co-operation in the animal kingdom is not only common it is also a crucial survival strategy, which we humans would be wise to learn.

Now according to experts this is happening throughout the animal kingdom, because all birds, and mammals, as well as Octopuses, along with so many other species that it is practically impossible to list them all here they all appear to be a great deal smarter than we would have ever thought possible.

The following is an excerpt from the Cambridge Declaration of Consciousness. (Which is a prestigious, official recognition of animal sentience) which was signed in the United Kingdom in 2012 by fifteen leading scientists, and was overseen by Stephen Hawkins.

The field of Consciousness research is rapidly evolving, and therefore calls for a periodic re-evaluation of previously held preconceptions in this field, because birds appear to offer a striking case of parallel evolution of Consciousnesses, and evidence of near human-like levels of consciousness have been dramatically seen in African grey parrots.

Mammalian and Evian emotional networks and cognitive micro circuitries appear to be far more homologous than previously thought.

Moreover, certain species of birds have also been found to exhibit neural sleep patterns similar to those of mammals, including r.e.m sleep and, as was demonstrated in Zebra finches, neurophysiological patterns previously thought to require a mammalian neocortex.

A Caledonian crow called Betty demonstrated human-like intelligence a few years ago by making complicated hooked tools from bits of wire to fish items out of tubes, now to put this into perspective, this is something chimpanzees (and most humans)are unable to do.

And just like Betty, chimpanzees are also cleverer than us in some areas, in a Japanese study to test short-term memory; numbers were shown on a computer screen before being hidden by white squares. The five year old chimpanzees who had been taught to count from one to nine in advance beat adult human's hands-down in remembering where each number was hidden. In addition, another study of long- term memory in chimpanzees gave some impressive results, thereby proving the average human are not so special after all.

Apes can also learn and understand sign language. And there is evidence that parrots don't just repeat words they also understand meaning. Dogs who wait patiently by the door five minutes before their owner gets home from work are not only expressing an awareness of time, but evidence of a sixth sense.

In addition, as a side note canines even align themselves to the earth's magnetic field when their "doing their business" so to speak.

Scientists have also recently discovered that not only are dolphins mathematical geniuses, the juveniles also like to chew and pass around puffer fish for no other reason than to get "high" with their friends which is not to dissimilar to rebellious youth behaviour in our own species. Furthermore, magpies, dolphins, great apes, and elephants can recognize themselves in a mirror just like us. And many studies show a very clear awareness of death in some species.

One of the most compelling and tragic was the behaviour of this young chimpanzee who lost her mother and died just three days later of a broken heart and leaves no doubt whatsoever about her understanding of death, because depression, grief, and mourning affects many animals in exactly the same way as us.

Other researchers from Kyoto University witnessed two grieving chimpanzee mothers carrying their dead babies for sixty-eight and nineteen days respectively after they died, as though they couldn't bear to say goodbye.

So it's simply "arrogant and wrong" for us to assume that we are the only animal species on this planet in which grief has evolved, elephants are especially known to grieve after the loss of a loved one. They mourn the dead by touching the bones or circling the body. Some researchers have suggested they may even relive memories and understand death in the same way we do.

Videos of animals exhibiting "human like behaviour" have gone viral on Youtube. Among them are a herd of buffaloes that get revenge on a pride of lions.

A heroic dog who risks his own life to drag his unconscious companion from the freeway, a baby elephant who cried real tears for five hours after his mother attacked and rejected him, and a cat mourning the loss of a friend. Nevertheless, sceptics warn against anthropomorphism, (the misguided attribution of human-like qualities to animals.) They claim we must always look for another, more basic, explanation before claiming other creatures are as complex as we are.

A sceptic might suggest, for example, that if a rat doesn't want to hear its companion being tortured, this is simply because the rat is averse to the sound of squealing. One researcher offers a good debunking of this kind of argument, because he points out that he is also averse to the screams of a tortured man, but it's precisely because he feels empathy that the sound is so unbearable.

It is widely accepted that many animals display and feel a wide array of emotions including joy, happiness, pleasure, love, empathy, compassion, sadness, and profound grief. However, researchers argue these are not human expressions at all they are in fact animal expressions, and the reason we share them with so many other animal species is that we are animals too, whether we like to admit it or not. We must never forget that our emotions are the gifts of our ancestors, our animal kin.

Yet historically, humanity has always treated animals with great disrespect and cruelty, and nothing more than chattels for us to exploit, for food, work, "sport," protection, entertainment, and experimentation.

Judaism, Christianity, and Islam, alike all teach that humans were given the right to use (and abuse) Gods lesser creatures, rather than preaching a sense of responsibility and stewardship towards them. (They also teach peace and understanding to your fellow man yet none of them appear to be capable of achieving it because they're too busy fighting amongst themselves over which religion they believe to be right.)

The idea that we are not alone in feeling pain, anxiety, shame, and depression is therefore highly uncomfortable for humans. Because if we accept this, how can we continue to treat animals as we do, or go on believing we are superior? In any case, some may ask what right we have to superiority because we are the most destructive and violent species on this planet.

And one animal rights activist quite rightly argues we cannot overlook an amazing paradox. It's an odd but revealing phenomenon that a species, which so arrogantly prides itself in its alleged unique skills in reason and communication, has not, yet attained an accurate understanding of itself. And this advanced "intelligence" of humans is in the advanced stages of exterminating our closest biological relatives, along with millions of other animal and plant species, thereby ensuring that Homo sapiens will die as they were born in ignorance of its own nature and the other animal species vital for an accurate self-understanding. Now this is not what we want to hear, but maybe it's what we need to hear.

We need to work for a science of peace, and emphasize the positive, pro social side of other animals and ourselves. It's truly who we and the other animals are.

People who claim nonhuman animals are inherently aggressive and warlike are wrong, and when they use information from animal studies to try to justify our own cruel, evil behaviour, they're not paying attention to what we really know about the social life of animals.

Do animals fight with one another? Yes they do. Do they routinely engage in cruel, warlike behaviour? Not at all, when people say you're behaving like an animal it's actually a compliment.

We also need to debunk the myth of human exceptionalism once and for all. Because it's nothing more than a hollow, shallow, and self-serving perspective on who we are. Of course, we are exceptional in various areas, and so are many other animals.

Would it surprise you to learn that, like animals, trees communicate with each other and pass on their legacy to the next generation? One Professor explains how trees are much more complex than most of us ever imagined. Although Charles Darwin assumed trees are simply organisms, competing for survival of the fittest, the Professor demonstrates just how wrong he was.

In fact, the very opposite is true because trees survive through mutual co-operation and support, passing around essential nutrients depending on who needs it. Nitrogen and carbon are shared through miles of underground fungi networks, ensuring that all trees in the forest eco-system give and receive just the right amount to keep them all healthy. This invisible web works in a very similar way to the networks of neurons in our brains, and when one tree is destroyed, it has consequences for all.

The Professor also talks about "Mother trees" usually the largest and oldest organisms on which all the other trees depend. The Professor also explains how dying trees pass on a "legacy" to the next generation, by shuffling important minerals to young saplings so they may continue to grow. When humans cut down mother trees with no awareness of these highly complex "tree societies" or the networks on which they feed, we are greatly reducing the chances of survival for the entire forest.

We didn't take any notice of it, but dying trees move resources into the young trees before dying, but we never give them the chance to do so. If we could factor this crucial knowledge into our forestry industries, we could make a huge difference towards conservation efforts for the future. To read the full report on this and other relevant stories please go to true activist.com. So I'll ask the question again are we really the most intelligent animal on this earth?

Seriously, now I know just how daft that still sounds to some of you, but consider what you have just read, and then think about what we are doing to this planet. And the one question that still confuses me the most is if we do possess this so-called "superior intelligence" then how is it we don't seem to have the intelligence to use this "superior intelligence" intelligently? Because is destroying the earth an intelligent thing to do.

Of course not, but maybe all the other animals are happy enough to live on this world the way it is, without the need to build an artificial world to live in, and they respect mother nature and her laws. Unlike mankind who just move in and relentlessly take whatever they want, and they use up all the natural resources in that area, completely unconcerned about the consequences of their actions or the destruction they have caused. Then they just move on to another place and do exactly the same thing repeatedly until eventually there is nothing left.

Humanity needs to remember where we came from and how it was Mother Nature who created us, and unless we change, as we destroy her we also destroy ourselves. Humanity desperately needs to relearn how to live in harmony with nature once more rather than trying to control her. And there's one fundamental thing that we should have realized a very long time ago, and that is humanity will never be able to control Mother Nature because whether we like to admit it or not, Mother Nature controls us. And if you don't agree with that statement just have a think about the way, we behave when the really bad weather arrives.

(The flooding in Somerset at the end of 2013 for example) and of course let's not forget how we struggle in the winter. Because we are powerless to do anything about these things happening, and as I've already mentioned the bad weather is not only predicted to become more severe but also more frequent.

We also need to realise that every living thing on this planet is in some way or another connected to each other. For example, all of the world's micro systems, each of which is unique and are fundamentally crucial for all life forms that live on this planet to exist. And of course, despite what many people may choose to believe, this also includes humanity.

Because when it comes to understanding this planet, we are nowhere near as superior or as intelligent as we would like to believe. Think about the vast amounts of money we spend on studying other planets when we know so little about the most important planet in the universe, which is the one we all live on. Now let me give you an example if I may, of how these micro systems work and just how crucial they are.

In Yellowstone national park where they decided many years ago that it was time to reintroduce a pack of wolves. Although many people were at first against the idea, however, since the release of the wolves the natural balance of things in the park have returned to what they should be.

Because during the absence of the wolves the coyote population rapidly increased due to the fact they had no natural predator to keep them in check, and they were devastating the herds of rare deer and many of the other animals that live there. However, since the return of the wolves, the coyote population has gone back to what it should be. And surprisingly enough the deer population has actually increased, the beaver is making a very strong comeback, and also, thanks to the beaver's dams, the fish numbers are also steadily increasing, and all of this has happened thanks to the reintroduction of the missing link in this unique micro system, which was of course the wolf.

Then you have the Great Barrier Reef in Australia, which is the largest living structure on the planet because the reef stretches for over 2.000 kilometres along the north east coast of Australia, and is so big that it's quite clearly visible from outer space. It's also one of the recognized seven wonders of the natural world.

But the coral reef is a very small part of this underwater world, as little as seven percent. The remaining ninety three percent of this marine world also includes a wide and varied range of habitats, each of which is remarkable in its own way.

And beyond them are even more environments that are just as important to the reef, some are close to shore while others are inland and there are over one hundred different types of habitat in and around the reef, each with their own distinctive animals and plants.

Yet all of the places these creatures live are all linked to a huge deep-water lagoon, which lies between the coast of Australia and the outer reef, all of which are connected, and each one plays a vital role in the wellbeing of the Great Barrier Reef. And this reef is not just a collection of coral gardens, but are in fact a unique network of many and very different habitats, and has a complexity of life that is seen nowhere else in the world. All of which helps to make up one of the most complex and spectacular ecosystems on the planet.

Now roughly two-thirds of the seafloor is covered in sand, which is being constantly moved around by the strong ocean currents, and at first glance, this area appears to be completely devoid of all life. However, on closer inspection, there is life such as garden eels that live and hide in the sand, along with shrimp and fish which again like to remain hidden in the sand out of sight of any predators. Yet one predator appears to find them very easily, and that predator happens to be the stingray. This apparently is the largest member of the ray family, now the stingray has the capability of picking up even the smallest of electrical signals that are being given off by their prey, they can even detect the heartbeat of a fish that's buried itself deep in the soft sand.

However, this ability doesn't come without its risks, because if enough stingrays decide to hunt in the same area it attracts other predators that hunt the rays such as the hammerhead shark, which in turn attracts other species of shark that also like to eat rays.

But not all corals are reef builders, because some are soft bodied coral that make ideal nurseries for the young fish that get swept in on the strong currents, and as they grow bigger and stronger they gradually make their way back to the Great Barrier Reef. That's if they don't get eaten by predators such as the aptly named stonefish that partially buries itself and looks like a stone sticking out of the sand, and it just sits there patiently waiting for any young unsuspecting fish to swim within range, it then just sucks them into its huge mouth. There are highly venomous Stoke's sea snakes, which occasionally pass through as they hunt for food.

Then you have the pearl fish that looks more like a snake than a fish, which has a unique and somewhat strange hiding place because it hides inside a sea cucumber whose body is basically just a tube that sucks sand in through one end and passes waste out the other. However, the pearl fish doesn't enter the sea cucumber through the mouth end, because it is attracted to the odour emanating from the other end. And once it's inside it seems quite happy to share its hiding place with other pearl fish, now most predators won't touch sea cucumbers so the pearl fish are relatively safe in their somewhat crowded hideaway.

Many varied creatures come to the Great Barrier Reef from all over the world, this includes such things as the tiniest plankton (the start of the food chain) right up the ocean giants that feed on them, and is home to some of the greatest wildlife spectacles on earth.

The Great Barrier Reef is also responsible for creating lagoons, islands, and sea grass meadows, which incidentally also happens to be the only flowering marine plant. Sea grass also absorbs ten times the amount of carbon dioxide than any other similar sized land based plant.

This micro system is also home to thousands of other species such as the mantis shrimp and feather stars, along with over 1.500 different species of fish. One of them called the damselfish has become a farmer of sorts, because it grows its own food by encouraging certain types of algae to grow in their patch of territory, and it destroys the algae it doesn't want. And they protect their territory with a vengeance and they attack anything and everything that attempts to enter their territory (including deep-sea divers) along with any other marine animals that rely on the reef for their food and for shelter.

This includes various species of jellyfish, now jellyfish make up forty per cent of the biomass in our oceans, they also help circulate the nutrient rich water, and they play a vital role in the oceans of this world. And one species that's aptly named the immortal jellyfish is slowly becoming the most numerous jellyfish in these oceans, and this tiny jellyfish really does live up to its name because apparently they never die. Because it has the ability to change itself, back into a polyp whenever it wants to, so it never grows old. Therefore, this little jellyfish now has all sorts of scientists really excited, because they intend to discover and then copy the gene responsible for this amazing feat in their never-ending search for eternal youth. As if, this planet doesn't have enough problems already.

Right then let's get back to the Great Barrier Reef, there are the sea grass meadows that cover 40.000 square kilometres of the ocean floor and provide food for the dugong, that are surprisingly enough more closely related to the elephant than the whales, and dolphins they so closely resemble. The sea grass also supports many different species besides the dugong. However, the sea grass depends on the reef for the sand it lives in. And a great deal of this sand is provided by the huge shoals of parrotfish that eat the coral and a single parrotfish can eat its way through an average of fifty tonnes of coral every year, and the waste they excrete, is sand. Now this sand is constantly moved around by the waves until they became small mounds rising out of the water and eventually they formed islands.

There are roughly six hundred of these islands dotted along the coast, plants and trees have grown on the majority of these islands, thereby allowing other species to colonize the reef, and they have now become eco systems in their own right.

Some are used every year by the thirty eight thousand female green turtles; the record for the most green turtles to come ashore on one beach in one night is twenty six thousand. Now the green turtles are a summer visitor and she has travelled hundreds of kilometres as she heads for the very same beach she was born on roughly twenty-five years ago. And she hasn't made this journey on her own because she has thousands of her kind with her and they are all driven by the same instinct, which is to return to the place of their birth, and they are the largest breeding population of green turtles in the world.

And after their long and arduous journey, they take a few days to rest and recover. And the butterfly fish takes full advantage of the turtles rest period because they offer a cleaning service, by removing the dead skin along with any parasites that have been picked up on the turtle's long journey to get to the beach. Which of course, they use as nesting grounds, and they return three or four times over the next few weeks to lay their eggs. However, it seems they don't make this journey every year, because apparently they return every two or sometimes every four years to lay their eggs. Now each female turtle can produce an average of one hundred eggs at a time, which they then bury in the beach, now that may sound like an awful lot of eggs, but on average, only one of the hatchlings is likely to survive into adulthood. However, the good news is each survivor can live to reach the ripe old age of eighty, (although there are records of green turtles surviving for one hundred years) however they are also facing problems which I will cover later on. Some of these islands have also become nesting grounds for the twenty or so different species of seabirds that also help to fertilize the islands, and they arrive each year in their thousands to nest and rear their young, but without the Great Barrier Reef and the parrotfish, none of these islands would exist.

Now this giant reef consists of two thousand nine hundred reef systems, six hundred tropical islands, and more than two hundred and seventy thousand square kilometres of coral, and the reason for this enormous size is that the reef is sitting on a huge platform that is over two thousand kilometres long and around two hundred kilometres wide. Now this platform provides the reef with a perfect shallow water shelf to grow on, this reef is also fed by a huge current of water known as the East Australian current, now this is by no means a little trickle.

Because, this current can be up to one hundred kilometres wide and five hundred metres deep, and capable of moving over thirty million cubic metres of water every second. In addition, this current carries near enough everything that's needed for life to exist and survive on the reef, because planktonic animals brought in from hundreds of kilometres up and down the reef helps spread life to all of its many individual parts. It has also joined up this massive eco system to make it the largest coral reef on the planet.

And all of this has happened thanks to a tiny little creature that's not quite one millimetre in size and doesn't even look as if it's alive. Yet it has unbelievably created all of this, and that creature is of course the coral polyp that has built this colossal reef from the ground up. This reef could quite easily cover the entire land mass of Great Britain all two hundred and seventy billion square metres of it, and all because of these little creatures each one living in its own little box of calcium carbonate. Which is the creature's home, and they deposit it below them in order to grow. Now the coral are related to the anemone and they like the anemone also have stinging tentacles, which they use to catch their food.

They also use them on each other in their constant battles for territory. Now in good conditions the coral can grow up to five centimetres (nearly two inches) a year, which when added up comes to a grand total of one billion tonnes of calcium carbonate every year. However, this growth is very demanding on both energy and nutrients, and even if it was possible for the coral to eat constantly twenty-four hours a day they would not be able to survive, because the water doesn't provide enough of the nutrients and phosphates needed for the microscopic plants and animals to grow. This also includes the plankton blooms that are the very base of the food chain.

However, the coral has developed a very clever little trick to get around this problem. And it has done so by joining forces with a single celled alga called zooxanthellae, which is a very big name for a very small creature, because these tiny single celled algae have become incorporated into the coral's living tissue, and in doing so have become an integral part of the coral. And there can be up to five million of them to each square centimetre, now the corals waste products provide the algae with all the nutrients they need to survive. And in return, the alga creates oxygen and sugars by photosynthesising which in turn provides the coral with ninety-five percent of the vital ingredients that's needed for them to grow. And subsequently thanks to this unique partnership, the algae and coral thrive, and by having algae within its tissue, the coral has now become half plant and half animal. Therefore, it needs the sunlit waters of the tropics in order to grow.

However, if the water gets below a certain temperature the coral ejects the algae then when the water gets warmer they simply renew their stock.

And when the water reaches a temperature of twenty-seven degrees centigrade and the moon is full, the coral releases its eggs and sperm in order to reproduce.

And it has taken the coral roughly ten thousand years to create this incredible place, which is a very short time indeed when compared to some species.

And you have to admit that's not bad going for a creature that is less than one millimetre in size and a tiny little alga that have joined forces through necessity in order to survive. Along with the incredible amount of creatures that are now, completely dependent on what this "joining of forces" has created. This also goes to prove just how vital these micro systems really are; because they give our eco systems the support and strength, they need to survive, just like the spokes in a bicycle wheel. And of course, the more spokes we break or damage then the more unstable that wheel becomes, until it eventually begins "to throw a wobble" which is what the world is doing now before finally collapsing unless something is done to rectify this problem and to stop it from reoccurring.

However, for some unknown reason humanity's, "superior intelligence" can't seem to grasp, or thanks to the blindness caused by the constant craving for profit they just choose to ignore this concept and this is why we're in this predicament in the first place because it has taken us, less than one hundred years to put it all under threat.

Therefore, as far as I can tell humanity to this planet would be the same as a flea to a dog, which is nothing more than a nuisance and a parasite.

Please believe me when I say I take no pleasure what so ever in calling our species parasites, because it is a terrible thing to say about your own kind, and a shame to say the least, because there are an incredible amount of things we could so easily do to improve this world.

Now, can you name me one other animal that forces their own species into slavery, especially child slavery? In many parts of the world, they still use children as cheap slave labour, and some countries still use or in many cases force young children into becoming soldiers.

Some ant colonies use captured ants as slaves but they don't abuse, beat, torture, or kill them. In addition, many of them eventually become part of the colony.

Now then, can you name me one animal (apart from us) that kills just for fun? A cat with a mouse, possibly, a fox in a hen house, no, the fox just gets a bit excited and would probably return for the rest of the kill if given the chance. However, we are the only creatures living on this planet that purposely design and create things to kill for fun, or as we like to call it, "sport" because it makes it sound ever so much more civilized.

For example the shooting of grouse and pheasant, or the great white hunters (I have no idea why they called them great.) Who killed the likes of elephants and tigers just to hang their heads on the walls of their drawing rooms, or to use as a rug in front of the fireplace? Or in the case of the elephants, using its hollowed out foot as something to stand their umbrellas in, just to prove what important, and fearless, real men (and women) they are.

Sounds like big car small Willy syndrome to me But then what do I know? I'm just a fifty nine year old welsh old school biker. This of course makes me in some people's eyes the scum of the earth. But still superior of course, because as I dare say you already know some people are more superior to others.

That's fine because it really doesn't bother me in the slightest, nevertheless, unlike many of these superior people my life consists of more than what can I rip apart next for a quick profit? And not giving a damn about the consequences of my actions because unlike these people money is not my God, as I try to make money to live, not live to make money.

Furthermore, what other animal declares war on its own kind, and designs and builds weapons specifically to inflict as much damage as possible to buildings etc, or to purposely maim or kill their own kind?

Well the answer to that question is, just us. Now believe me I am not slagging off any of the armed forces in any way shape or form as I have nothing but the highest regard and the utmost respect for those men and women.

I couldn't even begin to comprehend what they go through, or the horrors they see and deal with on a daily basis, and I genuinely take my hat off to each and every one of them.

My argument is about man's greed and his stupidity, (mankind is by its very nature a greedy animal) because for some reason they either can't see what they are doing wrong. Or on the other hand, and sadly even more likely, is the fact that the majority of them really couldn't give a shit. Which is a very scary thought to say the least, especially when they come out with little gem's such as, I really couldn't care less because I'll be dead a long time before it has any effect on the world, so why should I be worried about it.

Now let's be honest we've all heard or even said this at least once in our lifetime, great what a philosophy to have, I bet their children must be so proud of them.

Fortunately, not all of humanity thinks the same way, because the philosophy that it won't happen in our lifetime is no longer valid. Because, in a minimum of twenty to a maximum of forty years from now 2013, this world will be dramatically changed and very much for the worse. Now there have already been many changes made to this world in the past forty years. And all of them to the (temporary) advantage of humanity and unfortunately, very much to the permanent detriment of every other living thing on this planet, including the planet itself, and of course, this will also eventually include mankind. All of which goes to prove just how selfish, arrogant, greedy, narrow minded, self-centred narcissistic animals humanity can be in the never-ending search for that all important profit.

Thankfully, many people such as Greenpeace, Friends of the Earth, the WWF, along with many other charitably run organizations are doing their utmost to get the message across that we need to change our ways. And they are trying their best to educate people on how to stop this needless destruction before it's too late.

However, as usual the mega rich "profit hunters" are doing their utmost to stop these organizations from telling the general public what is really going on around them. Because in reality none of the many changes that have been made were for the better, so we will have detrimentally changed this world forever in a mere eighty years unless we do something about it and soon.

Now a very good friend of mine whose name just happens to be Dai Merlin Davies sent me this phrase to put in here which is. We did not inherit this planet from our parents, in fact our children only loan it to us.

Which I think is very apt, and it also pretty much sums up what I am trying to say here. However, we also need to lead by example, and we need to educate our children (and ourselves) on how to look after and respect, this world and the many different creatures that live here with us, because as I mentioned every living thing on this planet is dependent on each other in one way or another. Now I might be wrong, and I dare say at least one knowledgeable person will say I am. Fair enough, that's fine with me, because at that point I would invite every one of them to sit down and talk to me about it.

Now can someone please explain to me why, with all this worry about global warming, and the end of the world is nigh. Why are they still bulldozing the Amazon rain forests at a frightening rate? Humanity need to get their priorities right, because the world is rapidly being destroyed yet the British government are spending huge sums of money on improving the internet connections to some parts of the United Kingdom because people are complaining the internet in certain areas is to slow? So it seems to me if trees gave off Wi-Fi signals, the world would have been put to rights many years ago.

It's just such a shame they can only produce something as trivial as the oxygen that's so crucial for life to exist on this planet. One single tree is capable of absorbing forty-eight pounds of carbon dioxide a year, yet despite all the facts, they still continue to hack them down.

The equivalent of three full size football fields, are being permanently destroyed every minute just to be burnt or buried because it's so cheap to buy, once it's been used for shuttering for the one up manship families new bigger patios to stand their new bigger patio heaters on, just so it's bigger and therefore (in their eyes.) Better than their neighbours, whose name just happens to be Jones? And why is that middle aged Botox riddled single woman, with her peroxide dyed blonde hair and her makeup put on by a plasterer still driving that bloody big thirsty four by four around the centre of London, when she is the only person that ever goes in the thing?

Plus the only time that vehicle would ever be likely to see any kind of mud would be if she accidentally dropped her face pack in there. Oh and by the way, that fur coat looked so much better on its original owner. Yeah you know who you are. Well the answer to that question is one up manship and status. However, the truth of the matter is how they so desperately want and need to look and feel important, by trying to impress people, with their don't you wish you were me sort of attitude about them. Well to be honest. No. I wouldn't want to be anything like you sad people, it sounds like our old friend big car small Willy syndrome.

I mean for crying out loud even outer space is now overflowing with our rubbish. There are over a thousand satellites orbiting this planet. In addition, there are over a million pieces of space junk floating about up there.

(And that's not including the smaller pieces mind) all of which are travelling at an average speed of eighty thousand miles an hour. Now on average sixty to seventy tons of this space junk falls back to earth every year, admittedly most of which burns up as it re-enters the earth's atmosphere, however some of it ends up hitting people's homes. And now there's talk of sending things up into space to try and reclaim some of it. However, the different countries are now arguing the toss over ownership because they believe it could be worth money, and also to stop the "opposition" discovering any "secret technology" that may be on-board so basically, the

Americans can only collect American stuff the Russians collect Russian stuff and so on. (So humanity can't even trust each other) although to be honest I cant really see how they can salvage any of this space debris because I'd have thought the bulk of it would burn up on re-entry? They now have to put shields on the rockets to protect them because outer space is so full of our rubbish. As is the sea, and everything, and anything else we can find to hide our rubbish in. Now that really is super intelligent, don't you think so?

Can anyone please explain to me why the big oil companies have now been granted permission to drill for oil in the Arctic, thereby immeasurably increasing the threat of extinction to the many already struggling creatures that live there? The polar ice caps are already melting and the temperature rising at an alarming rate. (Three times faster than anywhere else in the world) The arctic could be completely ice free in the minimum of twenty years to a maximum of forty years and that's it all gone permanently, unless something is done.

Now as I dare say you already know that the Polar Regions are in darkness for around six months of the year, and when the sun finally decides to show itself these Polar Regions go through one of the biggest seasonal changes on the planet. The Adelie penguins (whose numbers are now declining) start arriving, and they have swam six thousand miles to get there which I think is quite a remarkable achievement in itself, and they make this incredible journey for one reason only, which is to breed. And during their stay, the leopard seals will take an average of five thousand of their young just from this one colony alone. In addition, each Adelie penguin will consume an average of one point five tonnes of krill during their stay, which is a very small amount indeed and the loss goes completely unnoticed because an estimated three hundred million tonnes of krill live in the Southern Ocean during the brief Arctic summer. And the krill feed on the algae that live underneath the ice, and are the very start of the food chain.

And the humpback and Minke whales cover huge distances to feed on the krill, and then of course, there are the killer whales. (Which are members of the dolphin family) that also arrive there to feed on the Minke whales and anything else they can catch, although it's recently been proven that killer whales have a tendency to specialize in hunting a certain type of prey for example, one group may specialize in Minke whales, while another group may specialize in seals. Killer whales were originally named whale killers because the early sailors used to watch them hunting and killing whales.

Then once the ice has melted you have the arrival of the Arctic cod. And they arrive there in truly colossal numbers because they come in shoals that can be up to five hundred million strong, and the predators come from far and wide to feed on them because the arrival of the Arctic cod is the main chance for these predators to gorge themselves on this huge supply of food.

Also, as it becomes warmer the insects are able to feed and pollinate the flowers and plants that have somehow managed to survive the extreme winter, however there is one remarkable little creature called the woolly bear caterpillar that feeds on the plants so it can make its incredible transformation from a caterpillar into a moth.

However, this little caterpillar is also capable of doing one even more remarkable thing, because if it can't find enough food to allow it to make this incredible transformation, then it will quite simply crawl under the nearest stone where it will stay right the way through the unbelievably cold winter.

And as it gets colder, it stops breathing, then its heart stops beating until eventually its frozen, even its blood freezes rock solid. However, come the spring this incredible little caterpillar just simply thaw's itself out and off it goes again, as if nothing had happened. Now this can go on for many years and some of these caterpillars can reach a ripe old age of fourteen years. (Which also makes them the longest living caterpillars on the planet) before they eventually manage to change into a moth, which I think is absolutely incredible.

And in the spring, the beaches there contain the largest number of animals than anywhere else in the world. Now in the North Pole for five hundred miles in each direction, there is ice that's a few metres thick, but in the next few decades, possibly by the year 2020 scientists have predicted it could well be just open water.

And the Arctic and the Antarctic are also undergoing some major changes, because huge masses of ice that have lain there frozen for countless years are now beginning to melt. And the consequences of this ice melting will undoubtedly affect all of us and obviously not for the better, because as I mentioned earlier the Arctic is warming up twice as fast as the rest of the world.

Now over the past thirty years, the local population of polar bears have had some major problems caused by their health deteriorating and the resulting weight loss as finding their food becomes ever more difficult.

This in turn would mean that any cubs being born to an underweight mother would also be underweight. Which really doesn't help the cubs chances of surviving their crucial first year of life, because due to the ice melting much earlier than it used to its making life for these animals even more difficult, so the survival of any underweight cubs are very slim (no pun intended) to say the least. Also due to the Arctic summers lasting longer, the polar bears numbers are dropping so scientists are now fitting them with radio collars so they can keep an eye on them, and once a year they sedate them so they can check the bear's weight, and its general health.

The scientists have also enlisted the help of the local Eskimos or to use their proper name the local Inuit people who are using G.P.S monitors to map any new cracks or weak ice they come across during their hunting trips so the scientists can predict how the ice will change in the years to come. Because since the year 1980 the ice cover there has dropped by thirty per cent, and to make matters worse, the ice has also halved in thickness over the same period of time. So now, there are only a few metres of ice covering the majority of the Arctic, which means it could all melt away during the Arctic summer and the same thing could happen to the North Pole.

So in the not too distant future, the Arctic ice cover could well be a thing of the past, which will only be seen again in the pages of history books, which is bad news for the already struggling polar bears and walrus unfortunate enough to live there, and all in the name of profit.

However, some people see the melting ice as good news because it would make drilling for the trillions of dollars' worth of gas and oil reserves a lot easier.

Now in the year 2007 Russia upset quite a few countries because they attempted to claim the seabed there as their own, while other countries were also trying to stake a claim to it however, the Arctic has never been as important as it is today. And not just because of the huge gas and oil reserves, because also in the year 2007 and for the first time in recorded history it was all ice free, so the Northwest Passage, which is a legendary sea route around the north of Canada and Alaska was open.

And if it were to remain that way, it would provide a much faster and therefore a much cheaper route between the Atlantic and the Pacific oceans. However, the loss of the sea ice isn't just a problem for the Arctic, because as I mentioned earlier the state of the ice also affects the climate of the entire planet.

There's also another problem, because all the ice on the land is made out of fresh water, now these huge glaciers are slowly but surely making their way to the sea. And the Greenland ice sheet is the largest in the Arctic, with the ice being up to two miles thick in some places and it's six times the size of the United Kingdom.

And during the summer, melt water lakes form on the ice sheet and they have greatly increased in number in the last twenty years as Greenland warms up. And this melt water eventually works its way through the cracks and channels called Moulin's that can drop vertically for up to one kilometre or more, until it reaches the bedrock below where it then acts as a lubricant. That then helps the Glaciers slide along the land on their journey to the sea.

And one melt Water Lake that was three miles long and ten metres deep had ruptured the ice below it through its sheer weight, and within a few hours, it had been completely drained. And it had done so with some incredible force, because it actually lifted one part of the ice sheet up by a metre which in turn speeds up the flow of the glaciers, because the ice is now travelling at twice the speed it was twenty years ago.

Now the travelling speed of these Glaciers also affects our sea levels, because once they reach the sea they break up into icebergs, and in May 2010, seventy million tonnes of fresh water ice that had been sitting on the land for so many countless years broke away in to the sea.

And sadly this is now becoming a more common occurrence as Greenland's Glaciers flow with ever increasing speed towards the ocean, and every iceberg helps to raise the sea levels just that little bit more, and scientists are now predicting that the sea levels will have risen by as much as half a metre by the end of the century. This would be enough to "swallow up" a large number of the world's low-lying islands thereby increasing the numbers of "global warming refugees."

Now ninety nine per cent of the Arctic's freshwater ice is in Greenland, which you must admit is quite a substantial amount however, this is just a mere drop in the ocean, (pardon the pun) compared to the amount that's "stored" at the southern end of the planet. Because in Antarctica there's ten times the amount of ice, furthermore it's also the biggest mass of ice on the planet, however, one giant Glacier has retreated by four hundred metres in the last six years alone.

And thanks to the warmer winds now reaching the Northern side of Antarctica, the temperature has risen by three degrees centigrade over the last fifty years, which is ten times greater than the average rise on the rest of the planet. And because of this rise in temperature and the resulting loss of ice, the Adelie penguins that used to nest there in huge colonies are now declining in numbers and it seems they are now looking for new breeding grounds. Because the larger Gentoo penguins that used to nest further north on the warmer islands have now started to colonize the area in ever increasing numbers which proves its getting warmer.

Now the Antarctic continent is home to the world's greatest ice sheet, which is one and a half times the size of Australia with ice up to three miles thick, and it also holds seventy per cent of the planets fresh water, and if all this ice melts, the world's sea levels would raise by a staggering sixty metres.

Scientists are now concerned with the sea getting warmer and therefore accelerating the melting of the glaciers. Because seven major, ice shelves have disappeared in the last thirty years alone, due to the temperature of the sea rising by just one degree. Now one ice shelf that was three times the size of Greater London broke apart in the year 2002 and once that had gone the glaciers it had been holding back, started moving six times faster.

Now in the year 2008, an even larger ice shelf at the Southern end also started to break up and an area the size of Yorkshire, which was covered by ice up to two hundred metres thick. Is now only half its original size

The other half has now broken up and some of the pieces were over a mile in length. And of course, as I said each one helps to increase the sea levels just that little bit more.

And unfortunately the rest of this giant ice shelf seems destined to follow it fairly soon, and is the latest ice shelf to disintegrate in a wave that's been slowly travelling southwards, and has been playing a major role in the loss of ice from the peninsula.

And the next in line are the already weakening ice shelves that are currently holding back Antarctica's gigantic continental ice sheet, and it would only take a small part of this ice sheet to slide into the sea to cause some major worldwide consequences and all of this has happened in the last thirty years.

Now if all this ice melted away it would increase the sea levels by a metre, which in turn would create even more problems, because it would then threaten the homes of millions of people. However if all the ice on the poles disappeared it would raise the sea levels by an incredible seventy metres it would also increase the temperature of the entire planet. Furthermore, if all the permafrost in these regions thawed then it would release a huge amount of methane gas, which is twenty times more powerful than carbon dioxide, and if it was released it would increase the rate of global warming so fast that the entire planet would be completely devastated.

This just adds to my argument that these places really do need to be left alone by humanity. Because as I've already mentioned all of them are now facing a very real threat of extinction thanks to Global warming, and all this is caused by the greenhouse gases that were created somewhere else on the planet. Because the worlds ecosystem doesn't have any boundaries, so we need to realise that wherever we live our actions create repercussions on the entire planet, because as I said everything is linked and is responsible for the health and well-being of each other and is something we all share.

Because if all the ice there disappears (and as I said earlier it has been predicted that it will all be gone in a maximum of forty years) then unfortunately it will be the end of the algae and the krill which are the very beginning of the food chain. And of course let's not forget about that remarkable little caterpillar, because sadly they will all be gone forever, unless we change our ways and quickly. Now all of this could and most probably will happen in your children's and most certainly within your grandchildren's lifetime.

Unless something is done and soon, and as I mentioned earlier the big oil companies have applied for and unbelievably been granted permission to drill for oil in the Arctic! Even though they have already admitted that if or when, there is an oil spill and the odds are there will be, then there would be very little, or nothing they could do about it. Now the Arctic is one of the few remaining places on this planet that has been practically untouched by human hands, and remains as one of the last true wildernesses left in this world, along with the oceans, and I strongly believe it should permanently remain that way.

Now the Arctic has the world's shallowest ocean, furthermore, two million square miles of it was once permanently frozen. Unfortunately, nowhere near that amount now remains intact, which really doesn't help in the battle against global warming because the Arctic ice as you know also plays a vital role in regulating the world's climate, and therefore its temperature. However, global warming is rapidly changing things in the Arctic because as I said it's heating up at twice the speed of anywhere else in the world, and within our lifetime, there's every chance of it changing forever.

Now a surprisingly large number of creatures depend on the ice for their very existence. Therefore, if the ice goes then they become extinct which also includes the many microscopic creatures that as I keep saying are the very beginning of the food chain. It's also been scientifically proven that the ice in the Arctic Ocean is vitally important because it stops the planet from overheating, and that over eighty per cent of the sunlight that hits this bright white surface is reflected straight back into space. It also contains a substantial amount of all the fresh water on this planet. However, unfortunately in the last thirty years alone almost one and a half million square miles of ice has disappeared, which you must agree is a phenomenal amount to lose in such a short time.

Now in the year 2007 and 2008, scientists went there to conduct some tests, which included measuring the thickness of the remaining ice, this ice is normally over three metres thick, and the ice has to be a minimum of two metres thick to stop it melting away completely during the Arctic summer. However, the measurements only proved the scientists worse fears, and that was the majority of the remaining ice was less than two metres thick.

They also discovered the melting of the ice was actually accelerating so it has now become a vicious circle because as the ice melts then the temperature of the water in the ocean rise as the newly exposed water absorbs the heat, which of course leads to more ice melting.

Also as the Arctic's temperature continue to increase, it also accelerates global warming, because as the ice on the land melts it releases carbon dioxide and scientists believe that it could double the effects of global warming if all the ice disappears. Now there has been permanent ice cover in the Polar Regions for an estimated four million years. And during the Arctic winter once the sea starts to freeze, the edge of the sea ice can advance by as much as two and a half miles each day. Until eventually, over five million square miles of ice will surround the Arctic Continent thereby doubling its size.

Yet humanity has practically destroyed it in a very short time, but we are not content with that, because as I mentioned the big oil companies want to put the final nail in the coffin by drilling there for oil.

Now NASA have been using satellites for many years to track just how much ice is being lost each year, now in the 1980's the ice was melting at an average of three per cent every ten years. However, in 2013 it has increased to eleven percent every ten years. So in the not too distant future two million square miles of ice could quite easily disappear forever along with all the life forms that depend on it for their existence, and all thanks to man's mindless and constant craving for fossil fuels and profit.

Furthermore, it will also have a very detrimental effect on the entire planet and everything that lives on it which of course includes humanity, because the Arctic Ocean unbelievably, is also responsible for regulating the circulation of every ocean and sea on this planet because it acts as a kind of conveyor belt of currents.

In addition, it moves nutrient rich oxygenated water through the oceans of the world, which are crucial for life to exist. It also helps regulate the world's weather patterns by moving heat around the globe, so if the melting Arctic ice isn't stopped soon then, it will radically affect our global weather patterns, and of course, it will affect our oceans worldwide.

Unfortunately, according to a report that was published in November 2013 it states that even if the carbon emissions were stopped tomorrow, the Arctic ice would continue to melt. The extreme weather conditions would also continue to increase, and there would be some fundamental changes made to this world Including the increase in sea levels, and the resulting loss of land.

Also its been predicted that if all the Arctic ice melts then there would be a dramatic increase in the number of earthquakes due to the once frozen ground defrosting, and therefore becoming more flexible. Plus the tremendous weight of the ice pressing down on it will have gone.

And of course let's not forget about the twenty five thousand polar bears, walrus, and other creatures that depend on the ice for their very survival. Including the tiny anthropoids (small shrimp like creatures) that live under the ice in the Arctic Ocean and feed on the alga that grows there, so both of these creatures are the very beginning of the food chain and therefore their survival is crucial.

Now over ninety-nine per cent of space available for life on this planet is in the sea, and this water covers a total of one point three billion square kilometres, it's also the largest single ecosystem on the planet and is much larger than any terrestrial ecosystem. It is also the least explored, because unbelievably, we know more about the surface of the planet Mars than we do about this huge marine environment, therefore this micro world is earth's inner space. Almost ninety per cent of the ocean lies below one kilometre, and over seventy-five per cent are deeper than three kilometres. And the very deepest part is an incredible eleven kilometres, which is just less than seven miles so you could place Mount Everest in there and you wouldn't even know it was there.

More people have walked on the moon than have visited the deepest parts of the ocean. And at that depth, you would be entering a world of inky blackness and tremendous water pressure. Yet despite all of this, it's home too many weird looking creatures, and some of the most strange and unlikely things live there. And even though they make up the majority of creatures on this planet we really don't know that much about them as they live in a world of complete and utter darkness, yet even at the very bottom of the ocean, there's life somehow managing to exist on this abyssal plain.

Recent discoveries have astounded many scientists and it's given us a chance to look into another world, so how do these creatures manage to exist in such a hostile environment? And what allows them to survive in such a cold, dark, and hostile world?

Well in the north Atlantic as the sun sets, a large mass of animals appear from the depths to feed at the seas surface and there are quite literally millions of them. Which range from strange looking jellyfish with large stinging tentacles to jellyfish that just ingests their food directly into their bodies, and some of the strange creatures simply defy classification. Creatures such as the small fish that takes cover inside the body of a pelagic jellyfish as it attempts to avoid the large numbers of squid that also arrive at the surface to hunt for food, because at night there are fewer predators that eat squid.

However, of course, not all animals need eyes to hunt because spotted dolphins can use their sonar to find their prey in the darkness with surprising accuracy. But where did these night time feeders and hunters come from? Well many of them rise up from hundreds of metres below the surface, and each night right across the world's oceans an average one hundred million tonnes of these creatures appear from the depths and it's the largest migration of animal life than anywhere else on the planet.

And the reason for this mass migration is the vast amount of food that's available at the surface, and this abundance of food is there thanks to something that happens on a microscopic level, which is something I've mentioned before and that is photosynthesis. Because tiny algae and plants known as phytoplankton use light from the sun to turn soluble carbon into organic matter which is called primary production. The by-product of photosynthesis is oxygen, and the water is rich with this vital element, which is of course essential for life.

The oceans produce fifty billion tonnes of phytoplankton every year during the spring and in the north Atlantic if the conditions are right it's possible to see the phytoplankton blooms from outer space.

And as I've mentioned they form the basis of the marine food chain and are therefore crucial for all life to exist in the oceans of this world, now phytoplankton are fed upon by some tiny creatures that are known as zooplankton. And the most common of these creatures are called copepods, now these little crustaceans are just over one millimetre in length; however, they are also the most numerous animal in the ocean. And in the North Atlantic, one square metre of water is capable of containing more than one hundred thousand of these little creatures. And it's thanks to the huge numbers of phytoplankton and copepods that the larger deep-sea animals come to the surface each night.

Then as the dawn arrives this massive migration returns to the darkness deep below. Now at two hundred metres they enter the first layer of the deep sea, and at this depth, there's less than one per cent of the sunlight breaking through, the water pressure is now twenty times greater than it is at the surface, plus the temperature has now dropped to four degrees Celsius. Yet at this depth, there is a wonderful world of beautiful and bizarre creatures most of which are transparent, which makes them practically invisible in the near darkness.

Animals such as the nine centimetre long amphipod, which is completely transparent except for the two enormous eyes and its central nervous system. There's also a strange crustacean that lives like a hermit inside a stolen body of a jellyfish, which she shares with her offspring, and because of this, along with the way she propels the shell through the water, has earned her the nickname pram bug.

Also at this depth their lives the longest jellyfish of all which is called the giant siphonophores, its tentacles can reach a length of forty metres (one hundred and thirty two feet) although only a fraction of these incredible creatures migrate into shallower water to feed at night.

So what do the creatures that stay in the deep water feed on? Well they feed on something called marine snow, and this is a vital food source for all the creatures that live below two hundred metres. The snow drifts down from the surface of the ocean where it originates, and it's made up from the scales and leftover scraps from such things as the mackerel shoals that swim near the surface as they make a desperate attempt to escape while being hunted by dolphins and yellow fin tuna from below, and seabirds from above.

Therefore, these mackerel have nowhere to go, and this attack continues until the entire shoal have been eaten, so their faeces, along with any dead and dying animals, and plant life descend slowly to the bottom of the ocean and many creatures such as the sea spider depend a great deal on this marine snow for its food.

However, as the snow slowly sinks to the bottom of the ocean its nutritional value decreases, because the majority of the "good stuff" is eaten as it makes its long journey to the ocean floor. But the deeper you go the less oxygen's in the water so life begins to thin out, however the life that does exist there is even more bizarre.

Because at five hundred metres if looked at with human eyes there would be total darkness, and the water pressure is now fifty times greater than it is at the surface, yet these strange looking creatures have adapted, some of them have huge eyes that enable them to see.

While other fish have developed, light emitting cells on the underside of their bodies so when their viewed from below they are practically invisible.

And as the marine snow slowly continues its journey through the depths, at eighty metres, the pressure becomes eighty times greater than it is at the surface and the temperature has now dropped below three degrees centigrade. And the oxygen levels are now less than five per cent of what it is at the surface, yet life continues to exist. With creatures such as the vampire squid that have lived in these depths for over two hundred million years.

And some scientists believe they are the missing link between the octopus and other squid. And they have specially adapted blood cells that allow them to live in this low oxygen environment, however despite their name and menacing looks these vampire squid are quite harmless. And they grow to a size of twenty-eight centimetres (eleven inches) and any predator that fancies its chances of turning one of them into a quick meal are dazzled by an incredible light show, which confuses the predator, and the squid quickly disappears into the darkness during the confusion.

Now beyond one thousand metres where there is no light, life still somehow perseveres. Because oxygen levels have now increased thanks to a deep water, current called the great ocean conveyor, because when surface water enriched in oxygen by photosynthesis meets polar ice it sinks beyond the first one thousand metres and it flows towards the equator therefore, carrying much needed oxygen to the deepest corners of this abyss. And at this depth, the real monsters of the deep live. However, the problem now is although there's plenty of oxygen, there's very little food.

And the only light available is now produced by bioluminescence. And most of the flashing lights come from deep-water copepods and they provide food for the other deep-sea animals such as squid, or the evil looking anglerfish that uses a bioluminescent lure on its head to catch its prey. And like many other deep-sea fish it has developed an extendable stomach, because in this dark and cold place it could be days before they get their next meal, so many of the predators have developed bioluminescent lures to entice and catch their prey.

Now these lures come in a wide variety of shapes and sizes, the wolf trap angler has its lure hanging inside its mouth amongst some very formidable teeth; but some of the prey they hunt have developed some rather ingenious ways of escape.

For example, the deep-water shrimp confuses them by rapidly spinning around whilst releasing a quantity of bioluminescent glue that sticks to the predator therefore making it highly visible to other predators and prey. Now most predators can't see the colour red, so any creature that uses that colour would appear invisible to the majority of them because they can only see the green or blue lights that most of these creatures create. However, there is one predator called the dragon fish that has evolved red bioluminescent headlights just below its eyes and these are very sensitive to red light, and its prey very rarely see it coming at them until it's too late.

Now eventually the marine snow reaches the seabed, which is six kilometres down, the water pressure at this depth is now six hundred times greater than that at the surface and the water temperature is practically zero degrees Celsius, and it has taken the marine snow many weeks to complete this journey. And when it finally settles it becomes part of a huge blanket of soft sediment that is over one kilometre thick on the abyssal plain, and these plains cover a third of the earth's surface.

Now as I mentioned by the time the marine snow reaches its final resting place it will contain only a fraction of its original nutritional energy, therefore under these conditions you would quite rightly expect these plains to be completely devoid of all life.

However, even at this depth life still exists, because there are Deepwater sea urchins sifting through the sediment to survive, there are also abyssal shrimp that use their extended antennae to feel for any tiny particles of food that may be floating around in the darkness.

Now admittedly life on these plains may be a bit on the sparse side, however because they cover such a vast area, they are home to some of the most numerous animals on the planet. Fish have been found living at depths of eight kilometres and the rat-tail is one of the most commonly found species, and it has developed white spots around its eyes that are extremely sensitive to the slightest of movements, which is a vital requirement in the dark and dismal abyssal plain.

Occasionally a feast will arrive on the plain in the shape of a large dead fish or seabird, which doesn't remain undetected for long because the scent will soon be picked up by deep-sea conger eels and in these conditions a good sense of smell is vital, and could quite easily mean the difference between life and death. Because the scent will also be picked up by the six-gilled shark that can grow up to a length of five metres, now these sharks have been around for at least two hundred million years and are believed to be the ancestor of the more commonly known sharks.

But there are many other deep-sea scavengers, such as the deep-sea crabs, arrow tooth eels, and the giant isopods that are related to the woodlice but these are half a metre long. So within hours the feast will have been devoured, even the bones are eaten as nothing is wasted. Now when life was first discovered on these plains during the nineteen seventies many people were shocked and surprised that even in the deepest parts of the ocean just how many incredible, and diverse creatures were living there, so we need to realize that the oceans of this world are still a very much- unknown quantity. And is one of our greatest assets and of great importance for our survival, so we need to stop mindlessly destroying something that is so vital. Now bearing this in mind, can you just imagine the impact the Arctic oilrigs would have on the oceans of this world and the already struggling wildlife? It would be devastating, and that's without any oil spills, or man killing things for "sport" because they were bored, and there's nothing else to do, or they were just wondering if they would be nice to eat, because you can practically guarantee some one will try it.

Now the oil companies original intentions were to start drilling there in October 2012, but thanks to Greenpeace who are now trying to get the Arctic declared as a nature reserve so please log on to their website, www.Greenpeace.com sign their petitions, and if you could make a donation they would be very grateful. Now thanks to the actions of Greenpeace the oil companies cancelled the drilling for one year. However, it is now April 2013 and the oil companies are back again trying to drill for oil.

Now Russia has jumped on the bandwagon and is also drilling for oil in the Arctic Ocean, and they say that this oil will be "the saviour of the Russian economy" and they have stated that they can clean up any oil spills that might occur. However, they have also admitted if the oil spill occurred below the ice (which just happens to be the most likely place) then there would be virtually nothing they could do about it.

Furthermore, they haven't even got a "plan of action" in place to treat any of the animals such as the polar bears or walrus living in that area if they happened to be caught in an oil spill, so they would just be left to die. However apart from that, apparently, it will cost the Russian government seven hundred dollars for each and every barrel of oil they produce, which in today's market is five times higher than they could ever hope to sell it for, so how is that going to help the Russian economy?

The Entelligent Idiot

Now I'm no businessperson but how can the Russians see this as a viable business proposition, as it sounds more like business suicide to me because we already know businesses need to make a profit correct? Yet Russia will never be able to make any profit from this oil, unless of course the intention is to "sit on it" for a while in order to push the prices up, which really wouldn't surprise me in the slightest.

Now fair play to Greenpeace who once again were there drawing attention to what is really going on in a bid to stop the drilling, but unfortunately, for them armed Russian Special Forces soldiers were called in to stop them. And they arrested thirty of the Greenpeace activists for piracy as they were peacefully attempting to board the oilrig platform in an attempt to hang a Greenpeace banner on there, and the Russian Special Forces actually opened fire on them, talk about using a sledgehammer to crack a walnut.

Some thirty Greenpeace activists are still being held indefinitely in a Russian prison waiting to go to trial. (they have recently been released but are still awaiting trial) so again I would ask you to please log on to their website www.Greenpeace.com and sign the petition to the Russian government asking for all charges to be dropped against the Greenpeace thirty.

The WWF are also there and they have been busy taking DNA samples from the polar bears and walrus that live in that area so they can prove to the Russian government that these animals are actually a sub species. Which are completely unique to that area alone and therefore should be classed as protected animals, in an attempt to get them to stop the drilling.

Now did you know that despite a very common belief, the polar bear is not actually white at all? Because the skin of a polar bear is as black as the tip of its nose and the soles of its feet and the top layer of the bear's fur is hollow and completely transparent, and it keeps the polar bear warm by absorbing the sunlight into its black skin. The heat is then reflected back off its body where it's then trapped in the many layers of fur. Plus a healthy Polar bear would have at least twenty centimetres of fat to keep them warm, polar bears can actually overheat.

And even when viewed through a thermal imaging camera the polar bear is still virtually invisible because the only heat source they would see would be coming from the bear's nose and the bottom of its feet. And despite all of man's modern technology, we still can't equal let alone beat the thermal qualities of its fur.

Nevertheless, the Russian government are still refusing to stop the work they have undertaken; in fact, they are still actively encouraging it despite the fact it will cost them more to produce this oil than they could ever sell it for, which again makes me think they are only there out of desperation. And I believe the big oil companies have absolutely no intention whatsoever of stopping until they have drained every last drop of oil from this world.

And I dare say you could say the same for the coal and gas companies but then the big companies run the governments not vice versa. I expect the next thing to happen will be the arrival of the poachers who will go there to kill the walrus for their tusks thanks to the illegal ivory trade. Perhaps the workers on the rigs will do it to earn a few extra pounds when they get bored because I doubt very much if they'll be too closely watched.

Now Greenpeace and the WWF have been working in the Arctic Ocean for quite some time yet all of this has been kept very quiet, because I haven't seen or heard any reports about it on the television, or the radio. There's been nothing about them being there or the reason why they are there in any of the newspapers, until recently with the coverage of the arrest of the thirty Greenpeace activists. And some of the newspapers appeared to delight in the fact that they had been arrested on charges of piracy and appeared to class them as some sort of terrorists? Which seems a bit strange don't you agree?

I'll let you come to your own conclusions on that one, but to be honest we really don't get told a lot by the governments of this world do we.

However, why don't these big oil companies just call it a day and stop the drilling? Because getting at the oil, gas, or coal once they've found it, keeps getting more and more complicated and expensive to extract.

Come on let's be honest, everybody knows the Arctic circle is not the friendliest or most hospitable place in the world, also the reason these oil companies are there as I said earlier appears to be more out of desperation rather than choice because they are rapidly running out of options and places to drill.

In addition, I dare say the same thing can be said for "fracking" now fracking is an abbreviation of Hydraulic fracturing and it is widely used in America. Which the government now intend to use in the United Kingdom but they are up against some very strong opposition from the British public because not many people want it.

The French have already refused point blank to allow fracking to take place anywhere in their country and fair play to them for standing their ground.

And it should have started the alarm bells ringing in the United Kingdom. One very good reason why the French won't allow it anywhere in their country is the fact that fracking has a very bad habit of causing small earthquakes, and also polluting the water table and quite a few American people have recently won high court judgements against a few of the fracking companies due to these facts. Nevertheless, it's being called the "saviour of our energy needs" by the British government, (which strangely enough is what the Russians said about the Arctic oil) however the British Government said exactly the same thing many years ago when North Sea oil and gas was first discovered but nothing changed.

Plus the fact that the British government are as good as paying these firms to do the fracking and then buying the methane gas off them. Because the roads that will need to be built to cope with the heavy traffic fracking will create is to be paid for by us the taxpayer. And the £100,000 incentive (bribe) that's being offered to communities to allow fracking to be done is also going to be paid by us the taxpayer. So basically, the government are just giving these people their own money back to them.

However, the best is yet to come because the British government have also decided that the fracking companies don't need to have any insurance whatsoever to cover possible and highly probable water pollution, loss or harm to livestock, land, buildings, and wildlife. Because once again we the taxpayer have been volunteered to pick up the bill for any and all damage done.

The government are also trying to pass a new ruling that makes the fracking companies exempt from trespassing laws. So in other words there would be absolutely nothing we could do to stop them from fracking underneath our homes, schools or come to that anywhere else they decided they wanted to frack.

Maybe the government need to be reminded that this is our money they seem to be spending so freely and of course, the sand along with the "undisclosed trade secret chemicals" that it contains will remain permanently in the ground. Furthermore, this shale (methane) gas will not be lowering our energy prices in the slightest because the majority of it will be exported.

Therefore, we the taxpayers will end up paying huge amounts of money for something we don't really want and more than likely will never get to use. Plus as I mentioned earlier methane gas is twenty times stronger than carbon dioxide so any escaping gas (which there almost certainly will be) will just accelerate global warming.

So is it really worth the risk? And what I have written here is just a brief summary of the government's plans, for more information on this and other relevant topics please visit www.trueactivist,com.

Okay then, let's have a look at what's involved in this fracking shall we, the first thing they do is drill a vertical shaft straight down for between one and a half and two miles (three kilometres, ish) then they drill roughly the same distance horizontally. They then pump millions of gallons of water, sand, and special "undisclosed trade secret" chemicals down the drill shaft at extremely high pressure thereby causing the rock to fracture which in turn releases the shale (methane) gas that's trapped in the rocks. They then pump the gas up to the surface through pipes and they move up the drill shaft and repeat the procedure until they reach the surface, then off they go and start the whole process all over again.

Now quite a few people who live near these fracking sites in America have become very ill so they went to see their doctor, who on examination couldn't tell what chemical had made them ill. So the doctor contacted the fracking company and asked if they could please have a list of the chemicals they were using in the fracking operation in order for the doctor to eliminate them from the possible cause of illness list. Unfortunately, the company refused to tell the doctor anything about the "trade secret" chemicals they were using unless the doctor agreed to sign a confidentiality agreement. So basically, even if the illness was caused by the chemicals used by the fracking company the doctor couldn't legally tell the patient because of their hands being tied thanks to the agreement they had to sign. And the fracking companies can legally do these things because the American government has recently passed a law that now makes it a legal requirement, so it's a bit of a catch 22 situation.

Now some of these people have received compensation for their illnesses, but it was on one condition, which was they are not allowed to talk about it to anyone. Including the fact, they were ever ill or what the symptoms of the illness were and they are most certainly not allowed to discuss how much compensation they received however, some people do want to talk about it.

And have said it was very similar to having a really bad dose of the flu. The majority of the people living in this area in Pennsylvania have now decided to drink only bottled water after the water coming out of their tap turned purple and made them violently ill.

Allegedly, the fracking company agreed to do some tests on the drinking water in that area, and they were told the water was fit for human consumption.

In addition, they offered no explanation regarding the purple colouring, so the people living in that area hired a private firm to investigate further, and also to hopefully find the cause of this problem, but when they arrived, the purple colouration of the water had disappeared.

However, the private firm were taking some water samples from the tap in the kitchen sink when they noticed a rather large amount of bubbles in the water sample.

Therefore, they put a gas detection meter near the neck of the bottle and discovered the water contained an extremely high content of shale (methane) gas and when they lit a match near the neck of the bottle it burst into flames and burnt for quite some time, so they now had flammable water.

Now I know just how crazy that sounds and obviously, it's not a good thing. And the private firm stated that it could have been caused by possible water table contamination because these people get their water from a well that's two hundred and fifty foot underground. And the contamination could have been caused through the extremely high pressure used in the fracking process and that would also explain why the well has failed every water quality test over the last three years.

However, as I mentioned earlier many of these people have now won high court judgements against these firms so hopefully things will now change for the better.

Now more than half of the gas used in Britain is imported, quite a lot of it comes from a place called Qatar in the Middle East and the reason we import it is the fact that forty per cent of electricity in this country is produced with the use of gas. (Although we have our own North Sea gas) now the ships they use to deliver the gas are over a quarter of a mile long and they carry enough gas on board to run seventy thousand homes for one year. So in theory it sounds like fracking is a good idea however, as I mentioned earlier fracking has been known to cause earthquakes.

Now in 2011, the first fracking operation in Britain took place and it caused a small earthquake although as far as I know nothing was mentioned about it happening on the news or in the newspapers? Therefore, I would not fancy living in a house that's been undermined due to fracking. Nevertheless, because there's a lot of shale (methane) gas in the ground in the United Kingdom the politicians in their infinite wisdom have decided that it's an "acceptable risk." This of course in political language means ah well if it happens, it happens and it also makes me wonder just how many of our politicians are "involved" in one way or another with the fracking companies that will be carrying out the work.

However, of course you can near enough guarantee that fracking will not be "happening" anywhere near any of their homes. So they won't have to worry about poisonous flammable purple water coming out of their taps and possibly bursting into flames, or one of their many houses sinking into the ground because it's been undermined. At least in the coalmines we put supports in to stop the tunnels from collapsing. And when they shut the coalmines down, they filled the tunnels with concrete, so maybe they could pump quick setting concrete into each shaft once the fracking is finished but then that would mean a drop in the all-important profit so I can't see it happening somehow.

However, what I still can't understand is why the government doesn't just invest all that money into producing these new battery cars, and of course, the hydrogen cell cars that thankfully many of the big car manufacturers are now taking an ever increasing interest in, and are known to help the environment. And one manufacturer is just about to launch the first mass produced car that runs entirely on a hydrogen cell thanks to an increase in public demand, and also the realization by the car manufacturers that we are rapidly running out of oil.

And I believe the car manufacturers will eventually shutdown the oil companies because they are now starting to realize that they no longer need to use petrol or diesel. Plus the new hybrid cars have created a new environmentally friendly "sales angle" that many car manufacturers will use to its fullest extent in their advertisements and fair play to them. Now surely these oil companies must know this will eventually happen, yet instead of investing in the future of these new cars, they prefer to struggle on with their futile search for oil.

And all because the oil and petrol companies due to their profit related "blinkered vision" don't want to know and they just decide to bury their heads in the sand because in their eyes, they stand to lose billions of pounds in lost revenue, which of course they will eventually lose anyway. Because we all know it's only a matter of time before the oil runs out, yet they are still trying their utmost to hold back this new technology and have been doing so for quite some time, because the petrol and diesel engines have been obsolete for at least forty years if not longer. The Hydrogen cell, which is the next topic, has been around for a hundred and fifty years.

Apparently NASA only use hydrogen cells for most if not all of their equipment, which also includes the space shuttle because both the electricity, and the drinking water are provided by hydrogen cells, and I dare say NASA would have improved on and perfected it by now. So the hydrogen cell must be a safe and very reliable source of producing energy, so if it's good enough for them, then why aren't they more commonly used?

However, the hydrogen cell is by no means a new idea because it was first used around a hundred and fifty years ago. It was invented in 1839 by a physicist named Christian friedrich schonbein. And then a Welsh physicist by the name of Sir William Grove started to improve upon it. However, the first vehicle to be powered solely by a hydrogen cell was a twenty-horse power tractor in 1959. Furthermore, Daimler Benz and Toyota each produced prototype hydrogen cell cars in 1997, and one car was capable of eighty miles an hour and had a range of two hundred and fifty miles, however, I dare say that's been improved on since then.

Also Iceland apparently have now declared that every car, lorry, bus, fishing boat' etc. Will soon be running on hydrogen cells so fair play to them, so all we need now is for the rest of the world to follow their lead. Apparently, you can buy conversion kits to run whatever you drive on a hydrogen cell and they cost roughly about two hundred and fifty US dollars, so I will definitely be looking into buying one of them.

Also, as I mentioned earlier that thankfully more car manufacturers are taking an ever increasing interest in these cars, thanks to a rise in public demand. Which goes to prove my theory about people keeping on about something (nagging) then something will, eventually be done. And it's also been predicted that every vehicle will be running on hydrogen cells in the not too distant future, (it's nice to have a bit of good news for a change) however to be honest I'm not holding my breath although hopefully it's true. Now I do apologize for keeping on like a pub landlord at kicking out time, but what I struggle to understand is why our illustrious world leaders don't get together and sort it all out, because they all need to admit it has to be done, and done quickly.

They also need to put aside their differences and their childish petty little arguments such as yeah but you're polluting more than I am. If that's the case, then all the other countries need to join forces and ban all trade with the offending country until they have reduced their carbon footprint to the required level.

Honestly, they really are just like spoilt little children who have just been told that all the sweets in the shop are free, yet they will still fight and squabble over who has the most. Just spend a few minutes and watch them in parliament on the television, they really are pathetic it's just a shame their wages aren't as pathetic.

These people are meant to be discussing important matters involving our country and the world, yet they act like little children in a playground as they try their best to shout each other down. My advice to these people would be this. Get out of the playground, grow up, and do the job your paid mega money to do, and lead.

Now I know their job can't be the easiest one in the world. Although let's be honest they knew this when they took the job. However, let's be absolutely honest because the majority of them are public school educated and have no idea what its like to live in the real world. Because the bulk of them have never had to struggle to get something they wanted (except maybe exam results) and they are just there solely for the money, even though most of them are already multi-millionaires.

I wonder just how many of them would still be in government if they were on a minimum wage, or better still on a voluntary basis in "service to queen and country" with no expense account or second homes to play with.

They also have all of these so-called "top brains" to advise them on the best solutions to whatever problems that arise However, unfortunately it would appear that when you become the proud owner of one of these "top brains" then all common sense and logic have to be removed before you are allowed to use it. Because it would appear to a mere mortal such as myself, that they go out of their way to find the most awkward and unusable solutions as they attempt to rectify these problems (and usually at great expense to us the taxpayers.)

Maybe they are trying to justify the huge amounts of money they command for their services although half of the time, I don't think they can really be bothered, and they try to ignore it as they keep saying problem, what problem, and just bury their heads in the sand.

Now personally I find the easiest and simplest way of doing something is also usually the quickest, and sometimes we need to look at things with a childlike vision.

Then of course they have all that political and diplomatic twaddle to wade through which I must admit can't be the easiest thing to do at the best of times. Although what I believe to be needed now is for someone to go in with a bloody big stick and sort the lot of them out, because as far as I can tell the big super powers are the ones causing most of the problems. And the very same people are also the ones shouting the loudest against whatever solutions that are being offered, mainly because in their eyes they stand to lose the most. Which of course is complete nonsense because unless something is done soon then everyone of us will lose?

In addition, they either can't see, or maybe they just don't care that they are killing this planet, and of course everything else including us with it. I'm sorry but it's not rocket science is it. And I'm fairly certain that a surprisingly large amount of people believe Global warming to be nothing more than a fictitious story. Although I dare say, many of these people will soon change their minds when a large part of London and the Houses of Parliament are under water.

Still that's not a great loss really is it? (In reference to the Houses of Parliament) I reckon that's a bargain myself, it would also stop that bloody woman with her dyed blonde hair along with the rest of her kind driving around in their four by fours. So that's a definite bonus really isn't it? I dare say by the time they realize what's happening it will be too late to do anything about it, or there will be a last minute attempt made to stop it, but that's a bit like shutting the barn door once the horse has bolted. Ah well never mind just change the name from London to Atlantis and its job done, and no one will ever be any the wiser.

Let me give you an example of our so called "superior intelligence" if I may, now quite a few years ago back in the early 1980's there was a massive pile up on one of the United Kingdoms major motorway's, with hundreds of cars, lorries, motorbikes etc., all mangled up. Now the cause of this unfortunate accident was really thick fog.

Nevertheless, what do you think the people involved in this accident blamed for causing it? Well unbelievably, they blamed it on the motorway hazard signs for not telling them to slow down, because there was thick fog on the motorway. Honestly, talk about shifting the blame. But then humanity has always been rather good at finding someone or something else to put the blame on, rather than accepting the responsibility for themselves.

Then there was the person driving down the road in an automatic campervan who decided it would be a good idea to walk into the back of the camper to make himself a cup of coffee while the van was still travelling down the road, so obviously he crashed. Now what do you think he blamed for causing the accident. Well unbelievably, he said because it was an automatic he thought it would be safe to go and make his coffee because when he hired the campervan no one told him he had to hold the steering wheel and steer the vehicle at all times when it was in motion. Furthermore, there were no signs anywhere in the vehicle telling him any of the above.

However, the best is yet to come, because apparently he sued the suppliers of the campervan over the no signs thing and as unbelievable as it may sound, he actually won his case. Now that really is insane "superior intelligence" my arse that would be like someone jumping out of a skyscraper window because no one's sat down with them and explained how they can't fly.

Whatever happened to people using common sense, logic, and of course the most basic of things, which is of course our inborn natural survival instinct? Honestly, I've seen more intelligent woodlice even they, (instinctively) know when to hold on to something.

Now if man decided it was time to get off his high horse, got his head out of his arse. And got back into living in the real world instead of this "virtual" world he seems to be so obsessed with at the moment.

I know people who brag about having over two hundred "friends" on a social network site yet they've never actually met or spoken to any of them in the flesh so to speak. Which I personally think is a very sad way to live your life. Maybe their trying to stay in this "virtual world" in a feeble attempt to escape from the reality of what's going on all around them, nevertheless, as I said if man could get his head together then just think of all the incredible things he could do with this superior intelligence, if he only put his mind to it. I mean for crying out loud we've even been to the moon and back (well so they reckon) However, that's just mankind looking for another planet to live on, and I dare say to plunder. There are now plans to place some plant life on the moon to see if they will survive, this apparently is due to happen in 2015.

Nevertheless, if man did eventually sort himself out, preferably before it's too late to solve our problem. Then the scope is quite literally endless.

If you sit yourself down and have a really good think, about all the incredible things humanity has achieved it really is mind blowing. For example, taking a person's heart out and replacing it with another or even a mechanical one. And intelligent artificial limbs that work through the brains electrical impulses so the person wearing it can actually feel what they are touching.

Or the amazing things they can do in brain surgery, and now even complete face transplants. They've even managed to grow one person a new nose as the original one was too badly damaged because of an accident they were involved in; the doctors grew the new nose on the person's forehead. Wow, you know what I mean. How do you learn to do something like that?

Now I must be honest, on this one we really are the superior beings, we've even created artificial life as in robots, in addition if you think about it the humble computer, which we all now take for granted, is actually an electronic brain in a box, and are getting quicker and smarter by the minute.

There are talks going on at the moment about the incredible advancements being made in the robot industry, and how we could all have robots in our homes to do the cooking and cleaning etc, in as little as fifteen years. There are also plans to introduce "self regulating" driverless cars on to the roads in many of the larger cities in the United Kingdom by the year 2015. And now the military are also talking about replacing some of the soldiers on the frontline with terminator type robots, but apparently these robots won't be controlled by anyone as they will be "self regulating." So maybe the terminator films weren't so far from the truth as we first thought? I didn't think it would be long before someone came up with the idea of using intelligent robots as weapons.

Then there are the buildings and structures that defy gravity, and to me are quite frankly incomprehensible. And I've been seen on more than one occasion standing there scratching my head and thinking to myself how on earth, have they managed to do that. Which I personally think is absolutely brilliant because it gets the little grey cells working overtime trying to figure it all out, which is great stuff and credit where credits due.

Now I must admit we do have many things we really should be very proud of, and quite rightly so. Nevertheless, unfortunately for us we do have a tendency to wallow in our glory. We also have a very bad habit of leaving things until the very last minute before doing anything about it. We also have a tendency to go off half-cocked, and then making let's call them "temporary repairs" (bodge jobs to you and me) and sometimes thinking if the problem is ignored for long enough then it will quite simply go away.

However, unfortunately for us this doesn't happen, simply because there is only so much rubbish that you can burn, bury, or dump in the oceans, ground, and atmosphere before Mother Nature decides right, that's it, and enough is enough. Then she starts throwing things back at us, (the "wobble in the wheel") for example, the polar ice caps melting. Freak weather storms, which appear to be getting more and more frequent, and more severe. Plus the fish and all the other life forms, that are dying in vast numbers, each and every day simply because humanity has either over hunted them, polluted, or destroyed their habitat, in our never-ending search for a profit just like junkies desperate to get their next fix.

The Entelligent Idiot

And are more than willing to do whatever it takes to get it, including the destruction of anything, and everything that gets in the way and sod the consequences.

Humanity needs to realise that Mother Nature makes a very good friend, however she also makes an invincible and unforgiving enemy.

So humanity desperately needs to relearn how to live in harmony with nature once again, before it's too late.

Then we have the problem of over fishing the oceans, which really isn't helping matters because if we keep on fishing the oceans at the same rate as we are now. Then in a mere forty-years' time this is the maximum estimate, (from the year 2012) there will be no commercially viable fish such as cod left to catch because we have already reached and passed the maximum number of fish we could ever catch, or to use the technical term "to harvest". The Oceans along with the fish need time to recover from man's constant onslaught against them. Just imagine the vast size of the world's oceans (they cover two thirds of this planet) and you really would have thought it would be an impossible task to "empty" something that immense, However, humanity are getting there, and getting there very quickly.

The intelligent idiot oh, I really do think so, don't you? In addition, I really don't think the phrase there's plenty more fish in the sea is relevant anymore these day's somehow do you. And now the fish may well have yet another problem to contend with, because it's been discovered there are huge deposits of cadmium, copper, and precious metals in the hydrothermal vents that are found at the bottom of the ocean.

Now at the moment (2013) there's a ship called the James Cook, which is basically a floating laboratory, and it's conducting research in the Cayman Islands on some of these hydrothermal vents, which are the deepest ones in the world. Therefore, they have to use a specifically designed remote controlled submersible to collect samples from the vents, and also to collect any life forms they may find down there in order to analyze them, because these vents are found three miles straight down on the ocean floor in the Cayman trough.

Now these hydrothermal vents can be found all along the geological faults that run across the ocean floor and they rise up like miniature volcanoes, and they work by sucking the seawater in through the ocean floor under extreme pressure where it's then heated by the volcanic magma to around four hundred degrees Celsius.

(Seven hundred and fifty two degrees Fahrenheit,) then it's blasted back up through the vent, many of these vents appear at first glance to be white, however, on closer inspection, it was discovered that they were literally covered in pigment-less shrimp. These shrimp also happen to be blind because at a depth of three miles there is no sunlight so they have no need for either eyes or pigmentation.

They also found tubeworms living alongside the shrimp and the researchers were very surprised indeed to find any life there at all, simply because of the immense water pressure found at that depth, combined with the extreme temperature. Nevertheless, these shrimp and tubeworms are actually thriving, because they are feeding off the bacteria produced by these hydrothermal vents, so these creatures are completely unique, and can only survive on these vents.

However, as I mentioned the scientists have also discovered these vents contain very high concentrations of Cadmium, Copper, and precious metals and they contain far more of these items than anything found on land. In addition, because of this discovery, many mining companies have now become extremely interested in mining these hydrothermal vents because it's believed that over four million tonnes of copper lie in one area alone.

However, scientists are not sure if mining these vents would be a realistic and or feasible concept because of the depth and the high temperature. One scientist commented it would be like trying to mine an asteroid because although you can see it, it is practically impossible to get at it. Therefore, the search is now on for hydrothermal vents that are not so far down, and therefore much easier to reach.

A Canadian company intend to dig up the seabed around Papua New Guinea where they intend to send some huge machines down to rip up the ocean floor and pulverising the rock (nodules) that contain the minerals and precious metals along with anything else that becomes caught up by the machinery. Then they send it up to the surface via pipes, the company intended to start mining this year (2013) but they were told they could not do so because of an on going legal dispute.

Nevertheless, this company is very keen to get started, and are now arguing that mining at sea would be much less destructive than mining on land. Which I completely disagree with (being an ex-coalminer) because mining is by its very nature a destructive business, furthermore, the machines they intend to use to break up the sea floor look very similar to the ones we used to use in the coalmines. These machines were called Doscoe Miners.

And they also had the same huge rotating drums and the same interchangeable spikes (called picks) fitted to the drums. Now these are very powerful machines indeed and they don't take any prisoners, because it just simply rips apart and destroys anything and everything that gets in its way, because these machines will quite literally go through solid rock like a hot knife through butter.

I had the misfortune of witnessing one miner get killed by one of these machines, and as disgusting as this may sound they took what was left of him up to the surface in what appeared to be a couple of bin liner's.

However, obviously at the bottom of the ocean, no one is going to see the amount of damage being done by these machines, or the lasting effect it will have on everything around it. Which I personally believe would be much greater than mining on land. For the simple reason that, all of the detritus, which would be created by these machines, which would be a huge amount as they churn up the ocean floor, would make the water cloudy, which would greatly reduce the oxygen levels. This in turn would have a very detrimental effect on every living thing in that area especially the plant life and coral because they would have no other choice but to stay.

And of course, all of this detritus could travel quite a long distance because it would be constantly moved around by the ocean currents, before it finally settled.

There is also the risk of these machines tearing apart and maybe even fracturing the seabed that sits between the machine and the volcanic magma that lies below. And possibly, causing some volcanic activity and I believe all of this would go completely unnoticed.

Alternatively, in the case of any volcanic activity would be "completely unrelated to any work that's going on in that area" because I very much doubt if anyone in authority would bother to run regular check ups to make certain no rules or laws are being broken.

Furthermore, the company have made assurances that the disruption would be kept to a bare minimum. (Now we've all heard that one before) apparently, they intend to remove any life that's found on or anywhere near the area they intend to mine. They have also promised to relocate them back to their original home once the mining is completed. Which seems to be a bit on the pointless side to me because the area will be nothing like it was originally, plus the hydro vents, which these shrimp and tubeworms depend on, would have been destroyed, so how are these creatures meant to survive in the watery desert that's been created?

They also predict that the mined areas will have completely recovered from the ordeal within a "few years," and what's the betting that any relocated life will have also been long forgotten about during those "few years" of recovery. And then we'll hear the "well they seem happy enough where they are now" excuse as they greedily try to protect that all-important profit.

Now the British government are busy promoting the mining, and one British company has apparently received a personal "push" from the prime minister, but this firm intends to vacuum the pieces of rock called "nodules" off the sea floor, which will then be sent up a pipe to the surface so the damage would theoretically be kept to a minimum. Now the United Nations through its international seabed authority sells licences allowing the exploration and mining of the oceans.

I'm sorry but I really can't understand how anyone can claim to own the oceans or come to that, any other part of the planet. Now I was lucky enough to have been born in South Wales however, that doesn't mean I own the place, if anything I'd say Wales owns me.

Most of the mining will apparently be carried out around the Hawaiian Islands, now many countries have already purchased these permits, but there are still arguments going on over the averse affect it could have on the marine environment, and also any possible knock-on effects (the spokes in the wheel.)

Because the mining in some areas could last for up to ten years or more, there's also a debate going on about the monetary viability of the project, because the materials they intend to mine are corrosive, so the upkeep costs of the machinery used to remove these materials has to be taken into consideration.

It's also been argued that if there were any attempts made to move the shrimp and tubeworms from these sites then they would die. Also moving them would be no easy task because you couldn't bring them to the surface because they would die simply because they have evolved over the countless centuries to live in extreme heat and water pressure. Now because they are a completely unique species the scientists are very concerned for their welfare. And they don't want to take the risk of making these incredible little creatures extinct, which makes a nice change. Unfortunately, one professor stated that if these companies decided they wanted to mine in a certain area then they would do so.

He also said you couldn't really say to these companies that you can't mine here because the area is classed as inaccessible or off limits, although personally, I can't see why they can't set limits to where they can or can't mine, or better still don't allow any mining whatsoever.

Because another marine biologist said we do not own the oceans, and we must all share the stewardship, and look after the oceans and not exploit them, and I wholeheartedly agree with that person. However, the trouble with humanity is the more we learn about something the more the likelihood of its exploitation increases.

Now for a change of subject, we have people all over the world that are going hungry, and many are starving to death. Yet we still throw millions of tons of perfectly good food away each year, and that's not including the "surplus to requirement" fish. And a lot of this food doesn't even make it onto the shop or supermarket shelves simply because it's slightly bruised, or the tin has a small dent in it. Or maybe its shape "doesn't look quite right" however, all of it is still perfectly edible.

Bearing in mind when I lived in a cave in cheddar gorge I was getting the majority of my food out of the rubbish bins, so you can believe me when I say when you're hungry you'll eat practically anything.

Furthermore, if I was starving I really don't think I'd be too bothered about the presentation of the food, because it wouldn't be on the plate or in the bowl long enough for me to worry about it. Now I'm not saying we should give these unfortunate people mouldy or bad food to eat. But as I say this is perfectly good food being needlessly thrown away because the shops and supermarkets can't even give it away in case they are sued.

Which I personally think is absolutely ridiculous. When it could be used to feed the hungry, surely the supermarkets and shops could come up with some sort of disclaimer so they couldn't be held liable. And I think it would also save them quite a substantial amount of money by not having to dispose of all this unwanted food. Because we have now had to open food banks in many parts of this country that rely solely on donations from the general public for all of it's stock. Yet consumers in rich countries waste almost as much food (a total of 222 million tonnes) as the entire food produced in sub-Saharan Africa which is 230 million tonnes. The quantity of food wasted globally each year is roughly thirty per cent for cereals, forty to fifty per cent for root crops, fruit and vegetables, twenty per cent for oil seeds, meat and dairy products, and thirty per cent for fish. Uneaten food ends up rotting in landfill sites and are the largest single component of American solid waste where it accounts for almost twenty five per cent of methane emissions. And globally agriculture is responsible for over thirty per cent of total greenhouse gas emissions.

So now, hopefully, you will understand both my confusion, and my frustration, when I sit down and think of all the good things man has done with this superior intelligence. However, it just seems so strange to me that it has never entered man's head to look after and care for their own kind. Because so few people have to much while so many people have to little. But again thankfully not all of humanity thinks this way In addition, as I've said we are more than capable of improving this beautiful planet that we are all fortunate enough to live on, let's face it we have already proven we can do the job.

Furthermore, the technology to do so has been around for quite some time. Then of course, you would have that nice warm feeling inside, knowing that your children would actually grow up and live in a better, cleaner world. Come on can you just imagine the immense pride you would feel knowing that your generation had literally changed the world for the better. Man that would have to be the greatest day in anyone's life surely, and believe me it is quite easily within our capabilities. If only someone had the sense and foresight to reach out, and grasp it firmly with both hands. Because it's just sitting there patiently waiting for someone in authority with the guts to reach out and grab it and make a stand. And that person would live on in history as the greatest person that ever lived.

Of course, you're going to be met with opposition from a number of people, God only knows why anyone would want to oppose it, but you can guarantee some people will. Most, if not all of which will be profit related however, I also believe you would be rather pleasantly surprised at just how many people would be standing alongside you, and I promise you this, I would be stood there next to them shouting the loudest.

Now if the governments of this world were to tell the car manufacturers, along with the oil and petrol companies, also the gas and electricity suppliers that they had to perfect, and produce the battery and the hydrogen cell cars within a certain time period. And the same time limits could be given for the installation of the wind and water turbines, solar panels etc. and to make things better. Now by this, I don't mean genetically modified crops and such like; I mean actually improve this planet.

As I mentioned earlier you can run your car on a hydrogen cell and the emissions are water vapour, which is brilliant because scientists believe we could be facing a water shortage in the not too distant future. Because eighty per cent of the ice peaks on Mount Kilimanjaro have now disappeared and many large rivers no longer flow all the way to the sea.

And then we have the Himalayan Mountains that trap the water from the monsoon and turn it into ice that's released in the summer when the snow and ice melts, and the Himalayan Mountains are the source of all the great Asian rivers such as the Ganges, and the Mekong. Over two billion people depend on these rivers for drinking water and for watering their crops, but global warming is shrinking the amount of ice on these mountains so these great rivers could soon be under threat.

And we have already "lost" quite a few streams and rivers thanks to them being recycled through our taps. Therefore, the hydrogen cell may well be the answer to quite a few of our problems, so let's do it.

There was a person in America, who in the 1990's apparently registered a patent for a car that ran entirely on water, and this person was quickly offered one billion dollars for the patent by an unknown buyer. However, the inventor refused to sell it, and sadly, soon after the offer being made he was found dead. The recorded cause of death put down by the Coroner was accidental death by poisoning, which appeared to be a bit odd. Furthermore, when a family member went to the patent office and enquired about the water car patent they were told in no uncertain terms, that the patent office new absolutely nothing whatsoever about this "alleged" patent and argued that it never existed.

Apparently there are over four million similar patents for everything from generators that are capable of producing limitless electricity that provide their own power to work so they have no need of any external energy input one such device was created by a man by the name of Tessla and it actually worked. But the American government are seizing these patents or inventions because they class them as a danger to American security?

Here's another "strange" fact for you to think about which is when Henry Ford decided to build the model T car he had spent the previous ten years or so researching the best way and also the best materials to use to build it, and also the best fuel to run it on. And he came to the conclusion that the best thing to use was in fact Hemp.

Obviously, not the sort of hemp that people smoke (Dope) although apparently there is evidence that smoking dope can help in the fight against cancer and quite a few other diseases. However, the hemp Henry Ford intended to use was the same hemp they still use today to manufacture rope for naval uses.

However, it can also be used to make hemp paper because an acre of hemp can produce between four and ten times the amount of pulp than an acre of trees, and by changing to hemp-based paper could apparently help reduce deforestation by as much as half.

Now Henry ford also intended to make all the car panels out of hemp so these panels would have been a kind of plastic, yet they would have been a lot lighter at least half the weight. And they would have been ten times stronger than steel plus apparently they were biodegradable. He also intended to run the car on hemp bio fuel.

However, suddenly the growing of hemp in America became illegal so he had no other choice and he had to use steel; however, he still decided to run his car on alcohol rather than petrol. And strangely enough, prohibition was introduced shortly after, thanks to some anonymous person making a massive donation to the temperance league of America to highlight the dangers of drinking alcohol. Now I am not by any means saying this person was killed for his patent, or that Henry Ford was forced into using steel and petrol when he quite clearly did not want to.

So is this just a strange coincidence or manipulation? I will let you come to your own conclusion on that one

Although they both seem to be a bit of a strange coincidence, don't you think? Anyway, back to the plot, we just need to persuade the companies that I mentioned earlier, that it really is in their best interest, which of course it is, to embrace this "new technology" that's been around for so many years.

They could use their huge profits and bonuses. Maybe the politicians could donate some of the vast amounts of money they cream off us the taxpayer with their "expenses" claims to help fund these projects.

Because to be absolutely honest I would prefer to be poor and alive, than stinking rich and dead wouldn't you. These companies need to get the wind and water turbines, plus the solar panels, producing renewable and efficient energy also by a certain date, and then you're halfway there, now I know it's not going to be as simple as I make it sound, but the governments of this world are meant to be in charge. Therefore, they should do their jobs, take charge, make the new laws and whatever else it takes, (short of a war) and get it sorted out. Because if someone doesn't do it soon, then it could simply be game over for all of us, and we'd be joining the dinosaurs and the dodo on the extinction list which would be a shame to say the least, as I quite enjoy living, as I'm fairly certain the majority of you do? Did you know that Neanderthal man survived on this planet for longer than we have so far? And unfortunately for us, the way we are going it will remain that way, because unless something is done soon we are not going to be around to outlast them.

Now earlier I touched on the great things man has achieved, such as open-heart surgery, and transplants. Then as usual, he goes from one extreme to the other, the person in the campervan for instance, or the person that took a jet engine off an aeroplane, and attached it to the roof of their car and then decided to try it out.

Well a few days later the person was reported missing, and all the police found was a massive skid mark outside the person's house, and eventually they found the owner along with the car embedded in a cliff face a few miles away. Now surely common sense should have told either of these people that it wasn't really a safe thing to do.

However, the one thing these people appear to have in common is their total disregard for the planet they share with us and the other animals. Which now brings me to another thing I struggle to understand, I have never met a person that doesn't enjoy watching wildlife programmes on the television, yet how many animals have either become extinct, or are now on the critically endangered list? And this list is growing bigger by the day. The majority of which has been caused by humanity's total disregard for anything that stands between them and their constant search and need to make a profit.

They also appear to be quite happy to leave the mess they've created behind them for somebody else to clean up. Normally these people do so either off their own backs or through charitable donations, voluntary helpers and so on, places such as the Orang Utan and young elephant sanctuaries, the parents being killed because they couldn't get out of the way quickly enough as their habitat was cut down around them.

Alternatively, they are shot for so-called crop raiding, which of course have been planted by mankind who have encroached on the land these animals have lived on for hundreds, thousands, or even millions of years.

But sadly, as far as humanity is concerned, they are just "dumb animals" and it doesn't really matter whether they live or die because we no longer have any use for them and they no longer have anything we want.

Except of course for the poachers who kill them for their ivory, fur, feathers, tiger bones, powdered rhino horn, and so on, illegal ivory buyers are now willing to pay as much as ten thousand pounds for a small tusk weighing as little as four kilogram's.

And rhino horn which as I dare say you know is made out of a substance called keratin, which is responsible for making our fingernails and also our hair. However, the rhino horn now has a black market value of up to $65.000 a kilo because they are now so rare. The poachers get an average of two hundred pounds for a pair of decent sized elephant tusks. So the people that buy the ivory from the poachers are making a very hefty profit of nine thousand eight hundred pounds for every four kilograms of ivory they get from the tusks they buy.

These poachers are also killing leopards, and cheetahs, for their skins and tigers for their bones. Now how on earth any intelligent person can be naïve or gullible enough to believe that the bones from a dead tiger or some powdered rhino horn from a dead rhino is going to help them in any way at all is completely beyond me.

Now Africa and the wildlife that live on this continent have seen more changes in the last fifty years than it has seen in the last two million. This includes an ever-changing landscape along with climate increases, the majority of which is again thanks to humanity, because the human population that live there are now growing at practically double the global rate. And so becoming overcrowded, and wildlife habitat is being taken over as a result. However, there are people trying to help the creatures that live there because Africa is the greatest wildlife continent on the planet, and whatever happens there will have an affect on each and every one of us one way or another.

Now one animal that lives there has become the world's number one target for poachers. And it has been virtually wiped out thanks to them, and that animal is the black rhino. Which have become so rare that they are now under twenty-four hour guard in an attempt to stop the poachers attacks because the poaching in Africa has risen by a staggering three thousand per cent in the last five years alone? And as I mentioned black rhino, horn is now worth $ 65.000 per kilo furthermore, these rhinos have now become a very lucrative target for organised crime and it's also now known to be funding terrorism.

And the Vietnamese and Chinese medicine markets seem quite happy to pay whatever the asking price happens to be and they don't appear to be too concerned about where it's coming from. Even though it's been scientifically proven that rhino horn have absolutely no medicinal properties whatsoever. (So the people who pay silly money to get it may as well use their own fingernails and hair,) yet it has made every black rhino in Africa a prime target. Apparently, the southern black rhino have now become extinct, and people have also been breaking in to museums all over the world just to steal the horns off the rhino exhibits.

Now the majority of the remaining black rhino are being killed in Uganda and Rwanda. And it's now believed that the total number of black rhino left in the wild in Kenya is now as low as six hundred and unfortunately, this is the maximum estimate. So the people who are looking after them have now started taking DNA samples so when any rhino horn is seized they can check where it's come from and the person selling it will be prosecuted, personally I think they should be shot.

Because even though the black rhinos are being monitored twenty-four hours a day unfortunately, the poachers still manage to kill at least one rhino a day however. Conservationists' right across Africa have now realised that if we want to save our large animals from extinction then now is the time to do it because the human population on this continent has just exceeded one billion.

And many of the wild animals are now being hunted commercially for food, some legally and of course some illegally, because some of this bush meat is quite often sold as beef or goat. And millions of tonnes of it get eaten every year all across Africa and many of these species could well become extinct in the not too distant future. Also because of this hunting, many of the predators are now struggling to find food.

Because fifty years ago there were roughly half a million lions in Africa however, sadly today there are less than thirty thousand left. Although in one part of Africa, things are improving in a completely unexpected way because the lions had been killing the local livestock that are owned by a group of traditional Massia warriors.

Now as I dare say you already know, part of the Massia warrior initiation into manhood involves killing a lion. Yet the Massia who are cattle herders and they don't believe in eating any wild animals.

However, when the lions attacked the Massia livestock they obviously retaliated, now it has been said that nobody knows more about lions than these people, as there has always been conflict between them.

Now the Massia have a huge respect for all living things and have a great respect and admiration for the lions. And a few of them have gone against hundreds of years of tradition and they have now become the lion's guardians. Because they have joined forces with a team of researchers who have been putting tracking devices on the lions so if they should happen to stray to close to someone's livestock, their owners are informed and they move them in a bid to avoid any conflict between the two of them, which I think is a very good idea.

And thanks to the Massia's help this research has now started to take off and is beginning to spread to other areas and the scheme has now become a huge success.

However, this area is also home to the last eight hundred or so wild mountain gorillas that are left on this planet, and sadly, as you can tell by the low numbers that the gorillas are also under serious threat of extinction. Thanks to the ever-increasing number of people that have started cultivating the fertile soil that surrounds the mountain gorilla's home so the gorillas have become isolated on the volcanic slopes because they have now become practically surrounded by farmland therefore, the gorillas meet these farmers quite frequently.

Which not only increases the chance of poaching, but it also greatly increases the gorillas chances of catching our diseases because unfortunately they have very little, or no resistance to the bugs and germs we carry, and at one point the mountain gorilla population dropped to just two hundred and fifty and were extremely close to extinction. So the authorities had to make some changes very quickly in order to save them, so the boundary limits of this national park had to become very strictly enforced in an attempt to stop the farmers from spreading into the gorilla's territory.

And they now have dedicated teams of scientists that monitor them constantly, and the forest is now patrolled on a regular basis to destroy the poacher's traps.

There's also a team of vets constantly monitoring the health and wellbeing of the gorillas and the majority of this work is paid for by donations from all around the world. And thankfully, the gorilla numbers are gradually increasing and every year there are a few more mountain gorillas, which has to be good news.

Leopards also live in this area, now leopards are the most numerous and widespread of all the big cats and they cover almost half the world, and while the tiger is so close to extinction and the lions are also very much under threat. The elusive and secretive leopard thrives, yet no one knows exactly how many leopards there are in the world but it is known that if you added the total number of all the lions, tigers, and cheetahs and combined them all together the leopard would still outnumber them all. Now the leopard's camouflage allows it to blend in perfectly to the many different areas and surroundings they live in, it is also quite at home hunting on the ground or in the trees, and many people regard this beautiful creature as the perfect predator.

Now a leopard weighs less than the average human however, it is much stronger and faster than any human; nevertheless, this wise and extremely cautious animal would much prefer to disappear into its surroundings than face confrontation. This is a very sensible thing to do because leopards live a solitary life and their enemies outnumber them by twenty to one. Which may also help to explain why they live such a secretive and practically invisible way of life?

Because they quite often have to share their territory with humanity, however the leopard can quite easily avoid them and they have in fact been very much a part of each other's lives for millions of years.

And during that time leopards have been visiting villages practically undetected, so people appear to be very much a part of their world. Yet attacks on the village's livestock by leopards are an extremely rare occurrence, now the leopards that live in India are smaller but just as adaptable and wary and they really do need to be, because there are tigers, wolves, bears, hyenas and lions and all of them are on the lookout for an easy meal.

And the Indian leopard just like it's African cousin also likes to visit the villages at night, and again it does so completely unnoticed. Even the livestock don't seem to be aware of its presence as the leopard just casually patrols the village as if it owns the place, and it appears to be a very curious animal and likes to investigate.

Then there's the Amur leopard that lives in Russia and they look very much like the snow leopard but are in fact the same as the African and Arabian leopard with only superficial adaptations. Sadly these leopards are also in serious trouble and their numbers are now less than fifty remaining in the wild. And the reason for their demise is once again down to the poachers who are killing them for their fur and for their bones, Furthermore their food source is also rapidly disappearing as the forests are destroyed around them, now as I mentioned earlier leopards have an amazing talent of quickly adapting to live in this ever-changing world.

However, it's not always enough and they are now critically endangered in Russia, because the leopards have now reached the limits of where they can live.

Yet further south there are rice paddies and palm oil plantations which stretch to the equator, so most of the natural wilderness has sadly disappeared, but the secretive leopards still seems to be holding their ground and they have become the most widespread large land predator species left on this world except of course for us.

However, many leopards are now being forced to live in small patches of forest that are surrounded by hundreds of miles of farmland where they are persecuted by farmers who class them as pests, yet the majority of people don't even realise that leopards are living amongst them. And there are now rumours of city leopards living in Beijing, Mumbai, and Jakarta and these city leopards are living on stray pets, rats, and rubbish, there are also rumours of them living in the wild in the United Kingdom with stories of black panthers living in the woodlands and moors. (The beast of Bodmin moor) because many were kept as exotic pets, however when the law was changed around thirty years ago many of these animals were either put to sleep, or were given to zoos.

But many people believe that quite a few leopards were also deliberately released into the wild by their owners, who couldn't cope with the thought of their pet being kept in a zoo and of course, some of them just simply escaped, and as you know, it's a well-known fact that the leopard is a very adaptable natural survivor.

Let's go back to the area of Africa and the mountain gorillas I mentioned earlier because unfortunately, the elephant population in that area were also having similar problems to the gorillas, and a large number of them died in a severe drought, simply because they couldn't go anywhere because like the mountain gorillas they were surrounded by farmland and roads. And then someone came up with the simple yet very effective idea of putting some underpasses in for the elephants to use so they could cross the roads without the dangers of getting hit by a car or one of the many logging lorries that are also operating in that area. So these underpasses have now become a vital lifeline for these elephants

This also goes to prove my theory that although the problem may well be complex, the solution to that problem doesn't also have to be so complex.

However, Africa's climate is also rapidly changing, because at the top of Mount Kilimanjaro, which is Africa's most famous mountain, unfortunately eighty per cent of its permanent ice cover has now disappeared, and scientists have predicted that it will soon be completely ice-free, again all this is thanks to global warming.

Now a very strange looking animal called the Gelada Baboon have become the latest climate change refugees because these baboons live in the Ethiopian tropics, and they live at a height of four thousand metres, because these Gelada baboons have adapted to live in the cold.

And they were once found all over the African continent and at one point there were six different species of these strange looking baboons. However now there is only one species left because as the climate increases the grazing becomes increasingly more difficult for them to find so they have to keep going higher up the mountain to cooler ground in their search for food. However, they are rapidly running out of space and they will soon have nowhere left to go, as they get increasingly closer to the mountains summit. So unfortunately, these Gelada baboons seem destined for extinction.

Now Africa is the hottest continent and it is definitely getting hotter, now the Sahara desert is the hottest desert in the world, yet life still manages to survive on the edges of this ever-expanding desert, however, for how much longer they can continue to do so nobody knows. Because there are now twenty two million people who are also struggling to make a living on the desert margins. Now one idea to stop the deserts advancement is to plant a "green wall" of trees across eleven countries, which obviously isn't going to be the easiest job in the world because of the "political difficulties" between some of these countries. However, quite a few of the people that live in these designated areas and are not particularly interested in the countries political difficulties, have already gone ahead, and started the project in a country called Senegal.

So hopefully this project will take off, but irrigating a five thousand mile long belt of trees is no easy task However, I dare say these people will find a way because they have now realized just how important it is to have the trees as part of their landscape. And one group alone has planted just over one hundred million saplings and fair play to them. These people are just one of countless groups and even solitary individuals, who are doing the same thing and are taking it upon themselves to reforest their bit of this great continent because trees are vital to this continent and also to the rest of the world.

Now in the Congo basin there is one of the most biologically important forests on earth. And not just because of the high concentration of animals and plants that live there, because it also happens to be one of the main sources behind the planets wind and rain.

Because every hectare of this forest releases one hundred and ninety thousand litres of water a year, this water then goes up into the atmosphere where its then transported all around the planet.

So basically, the heart of the world's weather lies in the tropical forests. However, thanks to the constant demand from Europe and China for hardwood, this and other forests are now under a major threat thanks to the enormous impact caused by the loggers as more and more tropical forests are destroyed. And scientists are now saying there is a definite and proven link between deforestation and the changing storm patterns all across Europe and America.

Furthermore, they predict the bad weather is going to become more frequent and even more extreme, and the damage caused by these storms will be extremely costly in both money and human lives and all of this will happen in the not too distant future. Yet it has just been discovered that an incredible fifty per cent of the Congo rainforest has been allocated for logging. Now the future of the rainforests has never been more critical for all of us and not just because they help control the weather patterns of this planet, it's because as I mentioned earlier they are also the planets lungs.

Nevertheless, we all know Global warming doesn't just happen on land, because Africa's practically surrounded by oceans, and many animals are now facing problems caused by the changing climate. And the green turtles that I mentioned earlier are one of them because the temperature of the sand she lays her eggs in also decides the sex of her offspring, and if it's high then they will be female, and obviously, if it's low they will be male.

So global warming will undoubtedly have a crucial effect on the turtle population, now the turtles play a very important role in this area as they help to keep the sea grass beds in check by feeding on it, which in turn helps the local crabs, and shrimp that live there.

Which of course in turn helps the local fishermen, so the locals have taken it upon themselves to help these turtles in any way they can, and they have opened a turtle rehabilitation centre to help any turtles that get caught in their fishing nets or happen to be injured by colliding with the boats etc. And since 1998, they have helped over eight thousand turtles to return to the sea, and fair play to them for all their hard work and commitment in helping these creatures. But sadly, these gallant efforts are only a partial solution because as I mentioned earlier how all the plants, animals, and even the landscape itself are all connected to each other in one way or another, and how they are all crucial to the entire ecosystem.

Therefore, it really is vital for humanity to use their "superior intelligence" to learn how to help these ecosystems survive. Because we really are rapidly running out of time, so it comes down to this generation to put right the many mistakes we have made over the years, so let's hope they manage to do so before it's too late.

Let's go back to the ivory poaching for a moment, because allegedly this ivory is being smuggled out via a new route in a place named Togo which is in Africa and apparently they smuggle it out of the country using shipping containers, because the security there are supposedly a bit on the lax side. However, there is something I find hard to understand and that is the fact that no one has used the so-called "superior intelligence" of ours to consider what the poachers intend to do once all of these animals are extinct? Which of course is very typical of humanity as it appears that all they want to do is bleed this world dry of everything, and anything, they can make money out of. And only when it's all gone, will they sit down and think oh shit what are we going to do now? Bang goes the lucrative Chinese medicine market.

Most of the elephants hunted by the poachers receive a terrible end, because the only reason they are shot in the first place is to stop them from running away.

So they normally get shot in a leg, now if the elephant is really lucky it will die instantly from a head shot. If not then while they are still alive the poachers just cut each side of the elephants face off with a chainsaw, so they get at the ivory or "white gold" as it's more commonly known and they then leave the butchered elephant to a slow agonizing death.

The poachers are now also killing the hippopotamus and the wart hogs for their much smaller tusks. Even the rangers who are there to protect these animals are murdered and the poachers then grotesquely mutilate the bodies in an attempt to frighten off the other rangers.

Most if not all of these rangers are volunteers yet they are willingly risking their lives on a daily basis in an attempt to help these animals. However, the only transport these rangers have are a couple of old pushbikes (and one of them doesn't even have a seat) and I believe the only protection they have are a couple of old decrepit guns and one of them had to be deactivated because it was thought to be too dangerous to use.

Now I know to some people this may sound like a sketch from some comedy show, but the reality of it is, these people so desperately need some help from somewhere. If you want to know more about the illegal ivory trade, then please visit bloodyivory.org and if you would like to make a donation to help in the fight against the illegal ivory trade then please visit bornfree.org.uk.

Right then here's a bit more about elephants did you know that one third of Africa's elephants live in the dense rainforests along the Congo basin? Now these forest elephants are slightly smaller than the savannah elephants, and their tusks have a pink colouration to them, and they are known in the trade as a rose ivory and because of this they are even more endangered than the savannah elephants. In addition, the poachers kill an estimated one tenth of them each year.

However, recent studies have proven that poachers are killing one elephant every fifteen minutes which works out that eighty thousand of these beautiful creatures die needlessly each year at the hands of the poachers. Now these forest elephants help to maintain the forests they live in by creating pathways, which other creatures use, and the clearings they create also allows the sun to reach the forest floor so encouraging new growth. They also help spread the seeds and fertilize the ground with their droppings, but unfortunately, they are now being pushed out of many parts of the rainforest thanks once again to the commercial loggers. And of course let's not forget the poacher's constant persecution of them for their rose ivory tusks because this ivory is much denser and therefore better suited for carving than the savannah elephant's ivory. And because of this, its value is astronomical because one pair of tusks is worth an incredible ninety thousand dollars on the black market and sadly, there are now only one hundred and twenty five thousand of these elephants left in the wild.

Now here's a thought maybe someone should put forward the idea of dehorning these animals? Now I know to some people this may sound a bit on the cruel or drastic side, although it must be said it has to be a damn sight less traumatising than having a chainsaw shoved into your face while you're still alive and then just left to slowly bleed to death in agony. I really do struggle to understand how anyone could be that heartless.

At least if they didn't have any horns or tusks they would have more chance of surviving because there would be no reason to kill them. (Some elephants are now being born without the ability to grow tusks) maybe they have realized that without them they will live longer so maybe they're not such a "dumb animal" after all (remember what I said about the stem cells?) However, there is still hope, because in Burma the forest

Covers near enough half of the country and it hasn't been touched for the last fifty years or so because of conflict amongst the people that live there, and it's also believed to be a sanctuary to some of the rarest and most exotic wildlife on the planet. However, the amount of this forest currently protected is only three per cent, now ninety five per cent of Southeast Asia's forests have already been destroyed and Burma contains half of what is left, and its forests would cover the United Kingdom.

And they are thought to be home to some of the most endangered species on the planet. Animals such as the sun bear, clouded leopard, and the rare Asian elephant because sadly in the last one hundred years up to ninety per cent of the world's Asian elephants have disappeared. And Burma's elephants are also very much under threat because they are hunted and persecuted by mankind. Now we all know that young elephants learn all the necessary skills to survive from the adults, so if the adults are killed then the herd falls apart.

The Entelligent Idiot

Well fortunately for these elephants, they live in a remote part of this dense and almost impenetrable jungle that stretches for over a thousand miles across the country and its isolation helps to protect these shy and elusive creatures from the poachers. However, humanity has now started developing the outer edges of this forest for farming because up to ninety three per cent of the people that live in Burma live off the land, and in the last one hundred years, the elephants have lost ninety-three per cent of their natural habitat.

However, that's not their only problem because the local farmers are shooting them in order to protect the land that had originally belonged to the elephants and of course they still have to contend with the ever-increasing number of poachers who hunt them for their ivory, and apparently also for their meat, however, I will cover that one later on. They also have another problem, which is the illegal capture of elephants for the tourist trade where they beat them into submission to break their spirit, and they are then trained to give rides to the many tourists that arrive every year, the elephants are also trained to beg off them. And it's been estimated that at least one quarter of all the elephants born in Asia will spend their life enslaved and in chains just for the tourist trade.

Furthermore, if it's not stopped and the Asian elephant is classed as a protected species soon, then Burma's elephants could be extinct in as little as thirty years.

Now as I mentioned earlier how the elephants play a very important part in the "housekeeping" of these forests, because like I said they help spread the seeds and they fertilize the ground, they also play a large part in the cultivation of new plant growth. Because as they move around the forest they create pathways and clearings that then provide the sunlight that's needed in order for the new plants to grow and they have in fact shaped this forest to look the way it does. And without the elephants presence this jungle would be a very different place indeed, which of course would have a knock on effect for all the other creatures that live there, so if the forests protected for the sake of the elephants.

Then everything else that lives there would also benefit which as far as I'm concerned has to be a good thing, because many people believe that these forests could be the last hope of survival for many creatures that no longer exist in any other part of the world.

However, Burma's forests are not just crucial to the animals that live there, because they are also of great importance for the entire planet. So a team of scientists, researchers, and some highly regarded wildlife film makers have been given permission from the Burmese government to explore these jungles in order to catalogue the many different species of animals, birds, and insects that live there, so the Burmese government can determine if the forests should be protected or not.

Also if they do decide it should be protected then they must also decide exactly how much of the forest will be protected because Burma rely heavily on its timber exports for its revenue, however it is vitally important to protect as much of these forests as possible in order to give these creatures a safe haven to live in.

And the researchers have already discovered two healthy herds of Asian elephants that are living and breeding in these forests, which is really good news because as I mentioned earlier they are critically endangered in so many other parts of Asia.

However, these people are not just there to protect the elephants because they are also trying to protect entire ecosystems, and also the forests diversity all of which will help to strengthen their case for its protection. Also on the top of their list are three animals that are rapidly disappearing from the rest of Asia, one of which is the endangered sun bear. Along with two extremely rare cats, one of them is the little known Asian golden cat and the other is the clouded leopard. And its believed these creatures are living in a very remote place called Salu which is also home to one of the most pristine and healthy forests in Burma.

Now as I mentioned this scientific team consists of some very highly regarded wildlife filmmakers, entomologists and biologists who are also hoping to discover some new species of insects and animals living in this unexplored forest. However, there are rumours that poachers have already targeted this forest as they increasingly widen their search for new supplies of ivory and such like for illegal black market trading. Now this forest covers six hundred and fifty square miles with many different animals living in different areas. And one creature they are desperately hoping to find is the extremely rare sun bear that have become the victims of deforestation in so many other areas of Asia and the entire population of sun bears has dropped by thirty per cent in the last thirty years. And it's also believed that this forest could well be its final refuge, so there is still hope, although the local people have been telling the researchers stories of sun bears being caught in snares and how the poachers cut off the hands and then sell them to the tourists for as little as a hundred dollars.

The local people also believe that the sun bears have practically disappeared from the forest as they are now very rarely seen; they also believe that the poachers are not local people and are a part of organized crime that's helping to fund terrorism. And the poachers have also been known to set fire to the forest in order to chase their prey into their traps, and apparently this happens on a regular basis, however as the locals said the bears are now "rarely" seen so there must be some still living in the forest. The researchers have already found a healthy colony of burying beetles that go in search of small dead creatures, which they lay their eggs on they then bury the corpse in the ground for their young to feed on.

And if it wasn't for these beetles then the jungle would be full of decomposing bodies, so they also have a vital role to play in the general housekeeping side of things, they have also discovered a rare species of blind snake that live and hunt mostly underground.

There are also over one hundred and fifty different species of birds, and the number is still rising, this healthy population of birds also includes the pied hornbill, now these birds are a very good indication that the forest is intact. There are also huge numbers of various species of butterflies, which helps to prove just how diverse this forest is. It also helps to prove that the forest is capable of supporting a wide variety of life, and it also proves there is plenty of food for the big cats to prey on, now the cats are the top predators and are vital, because without them the balance of life would be drastically affected. The researchers also discovered that a small town near the borders with Laos, Thailand and china, which is believed to be one of the major centres of wildlife trade, in Asia. And its very apparent that Burma's forests are its main supplier for this illegal trade of things such as tiger bones and skins, and you can quite literally buy anything in this towns market, from live forest animals to elephant trunks that have been cut up into convenient "slabs" of meat that are being quite openly sold as food. There are also leopard skins and bones, bear skulls, and all sorts of different bones from various species on sale for medicinal purposes.

This also includes bear gall bladders, and there's not a single animal that lives in the forest that doesn't eventually end up in this market in one way or another. And even though it's illegal it's all quite openly displayed and the researchers also discovered an illegal Asiatic bear farm, and these poor creatures have the bile siphoned out of their gall bladders twice a day, every day of their life. And one kilo of bile can be worth over two thousand five hundred dollars, which is then used in Chinese medicine, therefore, it is a booming business and there are row upon row of these poor animals in cramped cages on these farms. And this market has now been deemed as a major threat to the wildlife living in the Burmese jungles and the demand for this wildlife is steadily increasing. And of course the rarer the animal, the more valuable it becomes, so it's a vicious circle.

The Chinese and similar alternative medicine markets really do have a hell of a lot to answer to, so the Burmese forests are going to need some rigorous enforcement of the protection ruling if its inhabitants are to have any chance of surviving.

Because the researchers also discovered that, the golden cats and clouded leopards they were hoping to find are living and breeding in the forest. However, both of these cats are now extremely rare, and are therefore very much sought after by the poachers, so two of Asia's most endangered cats are in very urgent need of protection, there are also breeding pairs of sun bears thriving there. So perhaps in these forests there is still some hope for all of these beautiful creatures because as we all know their habitat is rapidly disappearing around them.

Now one area of forest is one and a half times the size of Wales, now this forest was once teeming with tigers and it's still strongly believed that they still exist there however, no one knows just how many there are. Now a tiger can quite easily travel as much as twenty miles in a single day and they are not the easiest creature to find, even though like many other animals, tigers tend to use the pathways and clearings that the Asian elephants create as they walk through this dense forest.

Now the last tiger to be caught on camera in Burma was around fifteen years ago and all across Asia the tiger is disappearing fast, now at the end of the nineteenth century there were an estimated one hundred thousand tigers living in Asia. However today there could be as few as three thousand left, the researchers also found more sun bears living and breeding in this part of the forest, they also discovered Shortridges Langurs which are a type of monkey, and they are only found in that part of the world. There are also large numbers of pig tailed macaques thriving in this rich and diverse forest, they also discovered some extremely endangered Hoolock gibbons living there, and these gibbons are also known to be very good indicators that the forest is undisturbed.

Now these forests are the most unexplored on this planet and the researchers are hoping to discover species of insects in the Tamanthi forest that are completely new to science. And in just one hour they found a staggering amount of already known insects including the Bombardier beetle and its defence mechanism is it shoots a mixture of really obnoxious chemicals out of its abdomen at just over one hundred degrees centigrade and if it hits you it really burns.

Which again goes to prove that this forest is completely unspoilt and packed with an incredible diversity of wildlife, however, it still remains under serious threat from the loggers as they get closer and closer to this pristine and valuable forest, now the Burmese government has pledged to stop exporting the wood from these forests. Yet they are still issuing contracts to private firms allowing them to carry out logging in so-called protected areas of forest. Furthermore, what makes matters worse is these new logging roads are now giving the poachers direct access to the areas they could not reach in the past, which now also includes tiger territory.

And as we all know, illegally caught tigers are killed and then used for traditional Chinese and other alternative medication. And as usual the poachers are not local people and these outsiders are more than willing to travel in their search for "new stock" for the medicine market that is now willing to pay twelve thousand dollars for a big tiger. So the demand is now enormous and of course, as I mentioned earlier the rarer they are the more valuable they become, so sadly the future of these beautiful creatures doesn't look to promising at the moment. Therefore, the researchers are hoping that the survey results that as I said have to be presented to the Burmese government will change the future of these forests, which will hopefully be granted a fully protected status in the not too distant future.

So the researchers head for the Megatha forest that is believed to be the stronghold of the tiger, however they have to be very careful where they walk because the forest pathways are littered with landmines that were left there after the war. Which really doesn't help in their search for this perfectly camouflaged animal, and while they continued their search, they discovered some large Indian civets and pangolins, which are insect eaters and were once quite commonly found in many parts of Asia until recently due to the demand for Asian wildlife.

They also came across a creature called a Binturong, which is the biggest civet in the world, and it's also known as the bearcat. Now the Binturong and the Pangolin are now both extremely rare indeed, they also found a huge variety of cats which means this forest must be full of prey for them to eat. However, there is still no sign of the elusive tiger as they have learned to fear humanity.

Now the Burmese government are trying to protect the tigers, and two hundred miles from the Tamanthi forest is the world's largest tiger reserve. Yet despite its protected status the reserve is littered with goldmines which are devastating the forest and also polluting the rivers, so the tigers future is again being threatened by mankind's constant search for a profit.

However, all is not yet lost because in south Burma the local people who are called the Karen, believe that animals such as the tiger have a spiritual purpose, and are keen to protect them, and the Karen people say there are still some big tigers living in that area. And one thousand miles away in another part of the forest tigers are finally discovered, so maybe things are looking up for their chance of surviving. They also discovered an astonishing amount of different moths, which also helps to prove that this forest is working as it should be. There are also a large number of different bats in this area, and one of them is called a megaerops, which is a species of fruit bat, however this type of bat are not commonly found in this area. And so far the researchers have documented more than fifty different species of mammal and twenty-two of them are carnivores, including seven species of cat in one area of the forest, which is a very rare thing indeed. There are marbled cats, which are normally nocturnal creatures and are very rarely seen, yet they feel safe enough to walk around during the day light hours also, the tiny leopard cat, along with the clouded leopard, even the rarer Asian golden cat, and her cubs seem to be completely at ease in the daylight.

The Entelligent Idiot

This is an obvious sign that they are not being hunted by poachers. The researchers also discovered the Malayan tapir, which again are also highly endangered, and these were the only tapirs they found in the whole of Burma? Yet they appeared to be quite content living and breeding in this forest, which is extremely good news as they have practically disappeared in so many other areas because of the rapid disappearance of their forest habitat.

So it would seem the tapir and the tiger have a home in the Karen state of Burma so if these remaining forests are granted a protected status then they have the potential to become a very much-needed permanent sanctuary where the tiger can live and breed in safety. Along with the many other creatures that are lucky enough to live in that area. So now, the researchers will compile a detailed list that will also include all of the species found complete with a list of all the insects living there.

And they will then present this list to the Burmese government along with a very long list of reasons why these forests need to be protected.

And hopefully thanks to all the hard work these people have put in, the forests will finally be granted a protected status and then the Burmese government have to ensure that it's upheld, and I really do hope it gets the protected status. Because it seems Burma's forests are the tiger's last chance of survival, along with the many other critically endangered species that live there with them.

Now for hundreds of years Arabia has been known as a desolate and unforgiving place where very little life can survive in such a harsh environment, however, there is one area of Arabia where life is thriving. And once a year this coast undergoes an amazing transformation, which in turn temporarily makes it home to more wildlife than anywhere else in the whole of Arabia.

Now all of this happens on the border between Oman and Yemen in a place called the Dhofar coast and along this coastline, the mountains rise one thousand metres above the shores. Yet this remote area is home to an amazing variety of wildlife, which thankfully includes the rare Arabian leopard, which is called the living ghost by the local people because it's so rarely seen.

There are Verreaux's Eagles that hunt in pairs in order to catch their prey which is a creature called the rock hyrax, whose closest living relative is the African elephant.

The Verreaux's eagle specializes in catching the rock hyrax and they have become near enough their staple diet. Now the hyrax feeds on the small plants and bushes that grow on the cliff face where they are safe from most predators; nevertheless, the eagles have devised a very clever way of catching them unawares, because the female will fly along the cliff face searching for prey. However, her partner is also approaching them, but with the sun at its back, therefore making it difficult to be seen, but the rock hyrax has a special blue retina in its eyes, which act like a pair of sunglasses so the hyrax stare directly at the approaching male watching it's every move. However, they soon discover that he was nothing more than a distraction. Because while they were all watching the approaching male the female had swooped in and made a kill, and they have to catch at least ten rock hyrax a week in order to feed themselves and their young, so these little cousins of the elephant are a very important part of a rich food chain. However, it's not just the mountains that are rich in wildlife.

Because just off shore is the Indian Ocean, which is also home to one of the rarest animals on the planet.

It's called the Arabian humpback whale of which there are less than one hundred left in the world. Now these Humpback whales are a unique species, because thanks to D.N.A testing, scientists have proof that these particular whales haven't bred with any other "outsider" whales for over sixty thousand years, so the last time they saw any others of their own kind there were Sabre toothed tigers roaming the planet.

So the scientists now believe they have discovered a completely new species of whale, and another remarkable thing they discovered is these are the only Humpback whales in the world that never migrate.

Now Arabia is so dry that not one single river flows permanently on the entire sub-continent, and the daytime temperature can reach forty-five degrees centigrade. Yet there are villages of goat herders making a living there, and of course the goats are under constant threat from predators. And packs of Arabian wolves have been known to break-in to the goat paddocks at night, sometimes wiping out entire flocks in a single attack, which of course is devastating for the goat herder.

However, the wolves don't always get to keep their kill, because there is one animal that will quite happily walk straight into the middle of a feeding pack of wolves, and that animal is the striped hyena, now this animal is more than capable of crushing a wolfs skull with just one bite. Apparently hyenas make more kills than any other predator (except of course us) and Dhofar is one of the few places on earth where wolves and Hyenas come face to face, there are also honey badgers, which normally forage for food on their own, but here they appear to prefer hunting in packs. And Arabian leopards roam this one hundred mile long mountainous area.

And the reason the Dhofar Mountains are so rich in wildlife is its position, which is right next to the Indian

Ocean. Now one predator namely the Arabian fox knows that in the month of May the female Green sea turtles will arrive just as they have for the past one hundred million years and that reason is to lay her eggs in the sand, all one hundred of them. And this is the only reason these turtles will ever come ashore, so once her job is done she heads off back into the sea, where hopefully, with a little bit of luck she'll avoid the fishing trawler nets until it's time to do it all again.

The Arabian fox who had sat patiently waiting for her to finish was now busy digging her eggs back up, because turtle eggs make a very nutritious meal for a hungry fox. However, this fox is not alone because as the number of turtles coming ashore increases, so does the number of foxes and these foxes can dig the eggs up much quicker than the turtles can bury them. And ninety percent of everything these foxes eat in their entire lifetime will be turtle eggs. Yet because the ten thousand turtles will lay over three million eggs between them all along this coast, it would take these foxes over fifty years to dig up and eat this year's batch alone, so the riches of the Indian Ocean also helps to feed the Arabian land.

And the sea itself undergoes a radical transformation as the warm surface waters are dragged away to the north by the Indian monsoon, which in turn causes cold water being pulled up from the ocean floor bringing oxygen and nutrients with it. And as the temperature drops the sea is being transformed into one of the richest in the world, as the microscopic plankton flourish and then an absolute explosion of life begins.

And fish from all over the Indian Ocean come here to feed, this also includes the graceful Devil Ray, some of which have travelled all the way from Australia to feed on this bounty. This is also the reason why the Humpback whales never leave, because they don't need to migrate to colder waters to feed, quite simply because the cold water comes to them. One other species of fish also arrives to share in this bounty and they are the Indian oil sardine, and they literally arrive in their billions, and a single shoal can be over three miles long and their sheer numbers help to confuse their predators. However, it doesn't help them against the world's most voracious hunter, which is of course humanity, as we catch half a million of them each year.

Now, although the Coldwater is good for the fish, it doesn't do the local coral population any favours. Because the water temperature has now dropped by ten degrees in a matter of weeks and the tropical coral is now being overrun by Coldwater kelp, which can grow up to fifty centimetres a day, (twenty inches) and are smothering the coral reef, however this will only be a temporary problem. The Indian monsoon finally reaches the Dhofar coast creating moisture laden clouds that head inland, and the air is now so humid that the clouds only need to touch something for it to release its contents.

So condensation settles on everything, and throughout the month of June it becomes one of the biggest weather systems on the planet, all thanks to the high cliffs trapping the clouds and relieving them of their moisture. And because of this there is more rainfall in that one area alone than the rest of Arabia combined; the Arabian Chameleon absorbs this water directly through its skin. And during this rain, the ground becomes so sodden that the snails that have been hiding in the soil for the last few months to avoid the heat start to emerge and the tree trunks become completely covered in snails as they search for a mate.

The land has now once more become a rich green paradise where a practically hidden Eco-system springs back into life, eventually the land can't absorb any more water so it drains away creating creeks and rivers, where the fish that have managed to survive the dry season by hiding in small pools, their numbers now start exploding. Some pools contain different species of fish, some of which are not found anywhere else on earth and this bounty of plenty lasts until September, then the scorching heat returns turning the land back into dust.

Scientists are now trying to get this area protected because they believe it is the last stronghold of the Arabian leopard, of which its been estimated there are now less than two hundred of them left in the world. So calling them critically endangered is a bit of an understatement to say the least. Now these leopards are known to be breeding there, as they live their secretive lives in the caves that have been formed in the cliff face. So as long as the Indian monsoon arrives each summer the Dhofar Mountains will remain home to the biggest diversity of life in Arabia and hopefully it will remain that way for many years to come.

Now the Vazantes in Brazil is home to a mix of land and water animals that are found nowhere else on the planet. And they range from giant otters that can grow up to two metres long (six foot seven inches) and huge Anaconda snakes, to Coatis (which are part of the racoon family) and Capuchin monkeys that are highly intelligent animals, and are capable of making and using more tools than any other monkey. They also have a very wide range of alarm calls for many different threats.

Now this area of Brazil has to endure some extreme weather conditions ranging from extreme drought and fire, to major flooding during the course of the year, and the floods come all the way from the Amazon. However, the flooding is not caused by the Amazon River. In fact, it comes from the largest expanse of tropical trees on the planet, which is of course the Amazon rainforest.

Because these trees are capable of releasing up to an amazing twenty thousand billion litres of water vapour every day, and this water vapour travels along the entire country and it's known as the Rio Voador. And some people refer to it as the "sky river" and when this "river" flows, it brings extreme floods and when it stops there's drought. So it's a very harsh environment to live in and it effects near enough every creature that lives in this huge country, however there is one creature that barely notices any of these changes, and that is the Capuchin monkeys that live in the Piaui canyons, because in these canyons it normally only rains for a few days a year.

Although the Capuchin monkeys do have a tendency to time the birth of their young so that when it does eventually rain, their offspring are big enough to take full advantage of it. However, other areas such as the rivers of the Pantanal will be subjected to immense flooding.

And the Giant otters start to make their preparations months in advance of the floods, and it involves the entire family. The first task is taking their young, which are called kits, for swimming lessons, because having strong swimming skills will be a crucial factor for their survival. The Giant otters also tend to dig several Holts just in case they have to abandon their present Holt when the monsoon arrives; therefore it's vitally important that the kits must be ready to face whatever comes with it.

And as the sun starts to get stronger over the north of Brazil, the Amazon rainforest continues to produce more and more water vapour that will soon turn into the monsoon rain. However, in the meantime life struggles on, and the Coatis are now taking their young out of the safety of the forest and on to the plains in their search for food. However there are many predators that are also thinking along the same lines. Predators such as the Savannah hawk that are very busy looking for food, and a baby Coatis would make an ideal meal for the hawk and its offspring. As like many of the other animals it waits for the monsoon and the time of plenty.

Now the Pantanal is the largest freshwater wetland in the world. And there are more Jaguars living alongside the Pantanal's rivers than anywhere else in South America. And during the dry season life is concentrated along the river banks, and the Giant otters are busy teaching their offspring (kits) how to fend for themselves in the water, along with improving the kits swimming skills in preparation for the oncoming Monsoon which will swell the Pantanal rivers with its deluge of water over the next two months. Until the rivers finally burst their banks and the landscape will be completely changed, and that's when the Giant otter kits are at most risk of drowning.

Or they are taken by predators such as one of the large population of Caiman, because more than half of the kits born each year are eaten by them, along with the Jaguar who, as it happens is also quite partial to Giant otter, and the Brazilian monsoon will change the lives of many different creatures all across the country.

Because thousands of miles away in the dry interior of Brazil there are just a few days of rain each year, yet it makes a big difference to the animals that live there. But until the monsoon arrives, the animals continue to find some ingenious ways to survive; the clever Capuchin monkeys have discovered a pool of water in the hollow of a tree. However, they can't reach it with their hands so they dip their tails into the hollow and they suck the water from their tails in order to get a much needed drink. Yet other parts of this huge country will be inundated, and in the centre the landscape will be completely transformed by the rain.

And one area that I mentioned earlier called the Vazante, which is a mixture of flood meadows and grasslands, which are surrounded by forests, but once the Monsoon starts, and the prevailing winds blow south, the grasslands will disappear for roughly five months.

Which for the Coatis, creates quite a few problems, because although they live in the forest they normally feed in the surrounding meadows that will soon disappear underwater, so they are busy feeding as they need to fatten up ready for the flood. Nevertheless, humanity will eventually want the land they live on so let's just get rid of them anyway, because after all it's only home to a bunch of dumb animals that we have no use for. And in a few years' time we can make a nice big profit when we sell the land for development. Logical no I don't think so, the way I look at it is this. All these creatures have as much, if not more right to live here as we do (remember the majority of them were here long before us, and hopefully they will still be here long after we are gone) Man may believe he's God with the ability, and authority to do whatever he pleases, but he isn't, and he hasn't.

Because despite what many people believe we do not own this planet, we never have and we most certainly never will. As for us through our own arrogance, claiming to be the owners would be the same as a flea claiming to own the dog or cat it happens to be living on at the time. Therefore, what gives humanity the divine right to destroy not only ourselves, but also every other creature that lives here, including all plant life the main example of this is of course the destruction of the rainforest, which if you think about it are as I said earlier the planets lungs. Because along with the phytoplankton (which are also the start of the food chain) that live in our oceans, between them they produce the majority of the oxygen we breathe.

Furthermore, it has recently been discovered that a creature called a Salp that lives on the bottom of the sea and are more closely related to humanity, than the jellyfish they so closely resemble. The Salps all link up together to create massive "daisy chains" which can be over a mile long, now billions of these creatures rise to the surface of the oceans every night to feed on algae.

This algae absorbs a huge amount of the carbon dioxide, which is continually being produced twenty four hours a day by us. But once eaten by the Salps the carbon dioxide is safely transported by them to the darkness at the bottom of our oceans, all four thousand tonnes of it each night. Now these Salps are rapidly increasing in number, thanks to the incredible abundance of food.

The scientists who have been studying these Salps also believe that these innocent little creatures could very well be the saviours of our planet. Because of the large amount of carbon dioxide they remove each night, therefore; it seems that the lower something is down the food chain the more important that something becomes, and not the other way around as we've always been taught. (This proves what I said earlier about everything having a purpose, and being the spokes in a bicycle wheel) which is fine as long as we don't become complacent and fool ourselves into believing we can carry on as we are, because the Salps will consume most of the carbon dioxide and we would be helping the Salps survive.

So it goes to show that just because humanity (through sheer arrogance and ignorance) believe something is no longer required, doesn't necessarily mean it's no longer needed. Furthermore, it also goes to prove that we don't have all the answers and we don't know anywhere near as much about this world as we would like to believe, because the truth of it is, we really know very little indeed. And we need to consider very carefully what affect our actions will have, not only on the planet, but also on the other creatures that are living here with us.

Creatures such as the incredible insects that can change into a completely different creature through metamorphosing from a caterpillar or grub and turn into the most spectacular butterflies, moths, and dragonflies, which is a process that never ceases to amaze me, especially the remarkable woolly bear caterpillar I mentioned earlier.

And this is just the tip of the iceberg of the many truly amazing things that we are lucky enough to share this planet with, yet we barely give them so much as a second glance or more often than not we class them as pests and vermin. And we also need to listen to the people who predicted many years ago that global warming would happen unless we changed our ways. Now I apologize for keeping on about this, but I really do believe these Salps along with so many other things are very important because as I keep saying, everything has its purpose on this planet (which hopefully I've explained.) Otherwise, they wouldn't have survived for so long and are not as dumb and surplus to requirements as we once thought.

In addition, of course there's the physical and the mental abuse we put these "dumb animals" through in the name of science, and for the good of humanity. Such as the laboratory, rats that are given cancer and other diseases just so they can be killed and cut open to study what effect it had on them, which is a complete waste of time because apparently they are nothing like us. Then there are the poor animals that have things such as shampoo and makeup purposely put into their eyes, in an attempt to stop them from stinging our eyes. And animals that were forced to smoke cigarettes, or force-fed to make them fat, just so the researchers could then test the latest "all new and improved" diet products on them.

Well I'm sorry, but if you want to lose weight then leave your four by four at home and walk to the shops, also try doing some exercise (maybe you can vaguely remember doing it in school?) Because humanity have now become the laziest animals on the planet and the majority of us have a tendency to drive everywhere, and most of us very rarely do any sort of physical activity.

Plus many of the things we do in our spare time are structured in such a way that you need to be sat down, for example game consoles etc. Furthermore, when you wash your hair shut your eyes, if you smoke then you already know the dangers of dying of cancer, or one of the many other smoking related diseases.

However, the difference is we know the dangers, (thanks to our "superior intelligence") and we also have the luxury of being able to choose for ourselves whether we want to smoke or not.

However, unfortunately for the laboratory animals they, as usual don't have any choice whatsoever. In addition, all their pain and suffering is completely irrelevant because it's for the good of humanity, and its okay to use these animals because they have been "specifically bred" for the job. Well I'm sorry but I disagree, and it certainly doesn't justify what they do to them, because I doubt very much if the animals in question have been clambering over each other in the rush to fulfil their dream of being used for testing before their cellmates.

Because they still feel fear and pain. Talking of cellmates they are also used for cloning, many years ago

I had to work in a research university as a builder, and there was this one large room full of some huge albino rabbits, and they were all identical and all diabetic, talk about weird.

Now I believe we should all adopt the same philosophy as the Native American Indians, Australian aborigines, the Inuit, (Eskimos) and the rest of the indigenous nomadic tribe's people, which is this. The earth is our mother, and she must be treated with the respect she deserves at all times, this is also very much a pagan belief. This incidentally is also very much my belief.

When these people kill something to eat they apologize for having taken its life, they then thank it for providing them with food, and we even look down on them.

America originally belonged to the Native American Indians. Yet they weren't actually declared and finally acknowledged legally as human beings until the standing bear trial in 1879. Then they were allowed to vote but it wasn't until the mid-1950's up until the early 1960's were they allowed to do so in every state in America. And Utah was the last state in the country to finally acknowledge their right to vote.

Furthermore the nearest they can get to living the lifestyle they used to, is on a reservation. And a lot of the time they are treated like second-class citizens, now the Native American Indian's have a saying, which is.

Once the white man has fished the last fish, killed the last animal, and poisoned the last river only then will he realize he has nothing left to eat or drink.

Which I think is very true, and it also pretty much sums up what I said earlier about what the poachers will do when they've killed everything that's worth money.

I have nothing but the utmost respect for the American Indian's, the Aborigines, and the Inuit, along with all the other remaining tribes people that are still managing to survive and live the life they want to in this ever increasingly hostile and violent world. Moreover, long may they continue to live that way of life, if that's what makes them happy then fair play to them. And I really do wish the very best of luck to each and every one of them. Because as far as I'm concerned if someone wants to lead a nomadic life style then that's fine let them.

Who the hell are we to say no you can't live that way anymore because this is the twenty first century, (although I really can't see what century we're living in has anything to do with how people want to live their lives?) Well personally I think if more people adopted the way these people look at life and this world, and even got rid of the stuff we don't really need we may have a fighting chance of making it to the twenty second century.

We need to get out of the virtual world that an incredibly large number of people choose to hide in, and we need to be brought back to reality kicking and screaming if necessary. Because we really do need to face up to our problems and find a way to deal with them, and the sooner the better. Although let's be honest we already know what has to be done.

Now I don't mean any disrespect to anyone when I say I don't mean all of humanity need to go back to hunting with spears, blowpipes, or bows and arrows to save the world. However, there has to be some very valuable lessons we can learn from these people. The first one I think would be teaching us how to respect this world, also the natural medicines they use, for example one of the world's most poisonous snakes the black mamba it's venom, once it has been refined produces a painkiller that's stronger than morphine, and has a lot less side effects. Plus the majority of medicines we take are plant based and one well-known company is now trying to claim the plant (herb) called Fennel actually belongs to them.

Furthermore, I bet these people have forgotten more about living and being happy than the majority of us will ever know. Now there's a place called Sarawak, which is in Borneo where the people of the Penan tribe live, and their numbers have dropped to two possibly three hundred maximum that still manage to live in the forest, this again is mostly due to the commercial loggers that are interfering with their traditional nomadic lifestyle.

Because the land the Penan people live on in this rainforest, is practically surrounded by the loggers and their bulldozers and they are slowly but surely working their way into the Penans territory.

And because in the loggers' eyes there's an awful lot of money at stake, the Penan people are having all sorts of problems as they attempt to stop the loggers from destroying their home. Now approximately two thirds of this rainforest have already been completely destroyed thanks to commercial logging in the past forty years, which means the nomadic Penan people have ended up being scattered into small groups that are now struggling to survive in this damaged and degraded forest.

And even though the government has promised to help the Penan people in any way they can nothing appears to have changed. In fact it seems to be getting worse and because of this out of the ten thousand Penan people only two or three hundred are as I said earlier still managing to live a nomadic lifestyle. And because they have been forced to live in small groups that usually consists of parents and their children the group very rarely exceeds more than forty people in total, and they now only have a territory of less than one hundred square miles. Now the Penan people believe if the rainforest is destroyed then they would also die.

Because they have no idea and just as importantly they have no desire to learn how to live anywhere else or any other way than they do now. Can you imagine the culture shock these people would get if they were forced to live in our world? I really don't think they could cope, and the Penan people have tried on numerous occasions to explain the situation to the loggers, but they built their roads and started logging anyway, and just chose to ignore the plight of the Penan people.

And because of the ground erosion caused by the loggers the Penan are having problems getting drinking water because every time it rains the rivers and streams they normally use are turned to mud. Yet despite their problems, the Malaysian state of Sarawak has still licensed seventy per cent of the forest for commercial logging. Now the government have tried to justify this huge amount by saying that it's crucial for the countries development, and they also say that the forest is being logged in a sustainable way.

However the loggers remove even the smallest of trees, and they then strip and burn anything that's left so the ground would be ready for the planting of acacia wood and palm oil plantations, Malaysia now produces fifty per cent of the world's supply. And it's thanks to our ever-increasing demand for these products that's creating these problems for the Penan people and of course eventually us.

The other problem is very few animals can adapt to living in these palm oil plantations so everything suffers, the Penan people once asked the loggers if they could take one of their tribe who was seriously ill to the hospital and the loggers just became aggressive and then beat them up (yet we call them uncivilised?)

Also, the houses that the loggers built to live in were promised to the Penan once they'd moved out, yet when the loggers did eventually move on they deliberately burnt the houses down just to stop the Penan people moving into them. Which was a bit spiteful to say the least, although I expect the Penan people would have only used them as storerooms; however, I very much doubt if the loggers were aware of this. Now as far as I can tell these people live this way of life because they choose to do so, and not because they have too. And I really don't believe, a lot of us so called "civilized folk" could truthfully say the same. Maybe that's the reason why so many people call the world we live in a rat race?

Another thing I struggle to understand is these tribes people look after each other, and they quite willingly share whatever food and possessions they have with each other so there's no hunger, homelessness or poverty, yet we still call them uncivilised? Yet we so-called civilised people thrive on one- up manship, and many people thoroughly enjoy having a I'm better than you attitude about them and will quite happily boast about the many possessions or the amount of money they have to less fortunate people as if it was some sort of a game where they score points.

We are also quite willing to kill another human being solely for financial gain. Whether it's invading another country for its oil, its gold or even for slave labour. Down to somebody killing another person just for a pair of "designer" trainers or jacket, it still boils down to the same thing, which is killing for gain.

And we are constantly told from a young age that we "must have" certain things in order to "fit in" with our peers, and how by owning these things would completely change our lives for the better and how much money you have is so important to your status.

You'd be surprised at just how many gullible people actually believe this crap, which of course is all complete and utter nonsense and is nothing more than media hype.

Just because these tribes people have no desire for the latest big screen 3D HD telly or the latest mobile phones and they don't want to kill anyone to get one because they are not even the slightest bit interested in our so-called civilised world or the shit that comes with it. And because we can't understand why they're not interested in our "super intelligent" world therefore, that makes them uncivilised? Which like I said is nonsense, if anything it should be the other way around, because we already know that "civilised" man is the most aggressive, cruel and self-centred animal on this planet.

Did you know that apparently there are still quite a few nomadic tribes people living in the rain forest that have never laid eyes on a white person, and some of them don't even know of our existence, and hopefully for their sake it will continue to remain that way.

And may they never have the misfortune of meeting us and our diseases. Unfortunately, with the rainforest, getting smaller, and man's greed for profit constantly getting bigger, the odds of them never meeting us are very slim to say the least.

Man already has the vast majority of the world to themselves, yet all these tribes people want is their little bit of forest which to them represents their entire world to remain untouched, for them to live peacefully in, and to be left alone to get on with their lives. And we even begrudge them that because apparently, they don't have the "relevant paperwork" that states they own the land, they live on. Even though they have lived there for as far back as anyone can remember.

(My my how very civilised we are) come to that does civilised humanity have the relevant paperwork that proves we own this planet? I don't think so somehow, simply because we don't own it, and never have or ever will. Therefore, it seems there's one law for us and everybody else has to do what we tell them, because we make the rules, because we are the "superior beings" which of course is complete nonsense for the simple reason that, no one has the right to tell people where they can live and what they can and cannot do. (Within reason) now there's one person employed on a full time basis to monitor these tribe's people, and that person is also there to make certain we don't disturb them.

I really do wish that person all the luck in the world because I have a feeling it's going to be needed, and also a well-deserved pat on the back for all the success so far. Now I bet none of the tribes people have to go and see a therapist because they just cannot cope with the "stresses of life" or they can't go out through the front door because they don't have a certain designer jacket the latest "must have" handbag, or trainers. Or maybe its because their mobile phone isn't the very latest up to the minute one on the market you know what I mean. Now admittedly some people really do need to see their therapist's because of nervous breakdowns, mental and/or physical abuse, and such like, which is fair enough and believe me I am by no means having a dig at them. Now I also know some of the illnesses these people have are psychosomatic, (all in their mind) but very real to them none the less so I can fully understand why these people would go to see a therapist.

However, of course as usual it goes from one extreme to the other, because you have these people who simply chip a finger nail and off they go crying to their therapist looking for sympathy. Did you know there are some people who genuinely believe that if you are not seeing a therapist on a regular basis of at least once a week minimum then there must be something seriously wrong with you? Now this seems to be a bit arse about face to me. It also strikes me as a very clever bit of therapy marketing and it also goes to show just how gullible some people really are, because let's face it a lot of it is self-inflicted, and please feel sorry for me as I have more money than sense, I'm bored, and I'm also an attention seeker. And the therapists are sitting there smiling and rubbing their hands together thinking of all that lovely money they'll make off them. Therefore, helping your fellow man and saving our species from extinction boils down to self-preservation and sod you jack, I'm okay; we really don't make things easy for ourselves do we.

Now considering man is a "pack animal," we really don't seem to be getting on as well as we used to with each other. Because I can remember when people were more than willing to help each other, and would quite often go out of their way to do so.

But now unfortunately, the majority of people walk around with an exaggerated swagger about them and trying their best to look all hard and mean, and they truly believe the world owes them a living and all they care about is themselves and how can they get something over on someone so they can use it to their advantage. Even the fashion models, or "super models" as they like to be called (because most of these stick insects cant spell anorexic) even they walk down the catwalk with a exaggerated swagger whilst trying to look all hard and mean, and these people are classed as role models for the younger generation? Maybe that's the reason we have so many young girls (and boys) in clinics as the doctors try their best to stop them from starving themselves to death, as thanks to peer and media pressure they attempt to look like these so called role models.

It would also appear that humanity is now becoming a solitary animal, because most of the time the majority of people seems to prefer going off into their own little world, with their headphones on listening to music or playing one of the many games on their phones etc.

I have seen on more than one occasion cars full of families and friends travelling up the motorway as they head of somewhere nice for a holiday, and every one of them is just sitting there in complete silence. Each one them in their very own private little world, as they play on their phones or other devices, with the most miserable look you could ever see on their faces.

As Albert Einstein once said and I quote, I fear the day that technology will surpass our human interaction. The world will have a generation of idiots unquote.

Maybe the pack is now to big because we seem to be constantly fighting each other over who will be the pack leader, to be honest I really am surprised that humanity has survived for so long. Seriously, we get one snowflake on the railway track and all the trains slowly grind to a halt, and the same principal also applies to the motorways and the roads, and then we all turn into headless chickens. Then you have people going into a blind panic as they start buying all the food in the shops and super markets even when they know, they don't really need it, and they'll end up throwing the bulk of it away.

Now what I can't understand is why we do these ridiculous things? Surely, with our "superior intelligence" we should have realized by now that winter is only a temporary thing and it happens pretty much the same time every year, and it's not the end of the world, as many appear to think. How many years have we had a winter? Yet we always appear to be so surprised, and being caught completely unaware of its imminent arrival.

Alternatively, in the case of the railway the wrong type of snow falls. You would have thought the authorities in charge would have come up with a "plan of action" by now wouldn't you? Unfortunately, for us, our winters also appear to be getting worse, and arriving later.

Some people blame this on global warming, but the jury is still out on that one but although we are being told there's no actual proof of this I believe the facts speak for themselves, and I think we all know which way the finger of blame is pointing. And if you are still not sure then I'll tell you its pointing straight at us.

We have also rather sadly acquired this, I couldn't care less sort of attitude about everything that's going on around us. Let's start with the way many people have very little, or indeed no respect for other people, or other people's property, belongings, way of life, or even their very life itself. The way people are injured or as I mentioned earlier killed just for the little bit of money they may have had in their pockets.

Or a pair of "must have" designer trainers or the latest mobile phone, or because they have a different skin colour, or believe in another religion, being in a different gang. Being in someone else's "territory" without permission, or simply because your face doesn't fit, and that's just scratching the surface.

However, what really winds me up is the fact that the people who commit these crimes genuinely believe there is nothing wrong in what they have done. And they honestly believe that if they want something, they can just go and take it, and they can do whatever it takes to get it, including murder. Because as far as they're concerned who's going to stop them? The already overworked and reduced in numbers police force will do what they can when they get the time. (No offence meant by that statement) These people even walk around with their exaggerated swagger bragging about what they've done, and will quite happily explain in great detail how they done it, and they appear to class it as some sort of achievement and a boost to their street cred.

Now I mentioned earlier that I have been a biker all of my life, and I have been a member of both back patch and side patch motorbike clubs. I also admit to doing a few naughty things during my life, but never without a bloody good reason. If you could just bear with me for a moment, I feel I must explain something to you.

I am lucky enough to have some very good true friends, and I am known for being a bit of a comedian and a joker. And, no one has ever seen this serious side of me (including myself) which I suppose goes to show just how strongly I feel about this world and what I have written here. Maybe I just needed to "get it off my chest" if you know what I mean.

Right then that's that out of the way, I apologize for going off on a tangent there. Now as I was saying earlier about the vast numbers of different kinds of life being wiped out needlessly by humanity, now a good example of this is happening to the crested black macaques. These macaques are a unique species that are only found in a place called northern Sulawesi in Indonesia now these macaques are very clever little monkeys that are full of character and mischief.

However, their numbers have been dramatically reduced by ninety per cent in the last twenty five years, these macaques live in the tropical rainforest, and a team of biologists that are studying these cheeky little monkeys have been following one troop for the past seven years.

There are seventy crested black macaques in this troop and on occasion they can be a bit of a vocal animal, which makes them fairly easy to find, which is good news for the people studying them however, being vocal quite often means bad news for the macaques because it also makes them an easy target for poachers.

One macaque was caught in a trap when he was just a baby and he had to bite his right hand off to escape from the snare he was caught in. And because of the loss of his right hand the troop he has lived with all his life have always treated him as an outsider, so unfortunately he is on the very bottom of the pecking order. Furthermore, the hunting has now put these mischievous monkeys on the top of the critically endangered list on Sulawesi.

However the macaques, and the forest very much depend on each other for their survival, because the macaques help the forest to regenerate by spreading the seeds they swallow when eating the various fruits that grow on the trees, and in return, the macaques get somewhere to live and plenty of food to eat. Now these little monkeys have evolved with this forest over thousands of years so they really do depend very much on each other for everything. But unfortunately, the monsoon season is undoubtedly the most dangerous time of year for these macaques. However, it's not because of the constant downpour of rain or the high winds that's causing them problems it's the local fishermen.

Because they can't go out to sea when the weather's bad, so they have to turn to the forest to make a living, and they do this by hunting and at the very top of their shopping list are the crested black macaques.

Now the macaque that gnawed his right hand off to escape from the snare was very fortunate indeed to have managed to do so, because countless other macaques unfortunately were not so lucky.

Now in a nearby town called Tomahon these rare macaques are quite openly being sold as food in the local marketplace, because the people of north Sulawesi have a taste for bush meat and hundreds of people descend on this market every week in their search for freshly hunted forest meat. This market also sells squirrels, rats, and snakes, people can also buy wild pigs and fruit bats.

The reason these people buy this meat is because this is what a lot of them ate when they were growing up and the demand for this bush meat is huge. However, the most sought after meat in this market unfortunately is macaque, which is quite expensive to buy because it's illegal to kill them because as I said earlier they've been classed as critically endangered. Unfortunately, quite a lot of the people who buy the macaque meat don't know the macaque are an endangered species, and the reason people quite innocently pay so much for the meat is because its classed by many as a delicacy, and people really like eating them because they taste so nice.

So the last wild population of these cheeky little creatures are steadily disappearing from the forest and sadly heading for extinction simply because they taste nice and people like to eat them. However, there are some people fighting the macaques' corner and they are doing their best to educate the local people by showing them the films they have made of them as they go about their business in the wild. They have also taken the local schoolchildren and some of the parents on a few field trips into the jungle to see for themselves how these cheeky little monkeys behave in their own environment. And also, to show them just how special and important to the forest these clever little creatures really are.

Most of these people have never even seen a live macaque, let alone gone to see them for themselves in the wild, so now these people have seen these macaques in their own environment and they seem to have thoroughly enjoyed the experience. So they now have a better understanding of not only just how close to extinction, but also just how important these monkeys really are to the forest, and hopefully this will stop them wanting to eat them, and to be honest things are now beginning to look quite promising for the macaques.

Here's another example, this time let's use the snow leopard, which is very high on the critically endangered list. So what's the best thing to do to help them recover? Yep, you've guessed it; some idiot who thinks he can make a nice little profit out of it, comes along and offers to pay some poor bushman a small pittance to show him where the snow leopard lives. Then he shoots it so he can sell the skin to some sad but extremely wealthy collector who so desperately needs to have one to add to his illegal collection of rare animal skins before they all disappear. And if this collector isn't willing to pay the extortionate price he's asking for it?

Then until he finds someone who is willing to pay the asking price, he just takes it home to hang on his drawing room wall, or maybe to use it as a rug in front of his fireplace, so he can show all of his chums what one looked like before they were extinct. And, how it's a terrible shame they're now all dead, because he can vaguely remember what a beautiful animal it was just before he blew a bloody big hole in it.

However the saddest thing is, this person actually believes they has done the snow leopard a huge favour by shooting it. Well thanks for that then, and if we need your help again we will call you, honestly we will. Now how do you explain to people like them that what they have done was wrong? Because when you tell these people you are actually doing your best to stop these, and many other animals becoming extinct they reply, oh I am ever so sorry, because one did not realize that one was not allowed to shoot them. In addition may one make a large donation to whatever the name of your cause is, as a way of an apology and compensation?

(In an attempt to get out of being prosecuted) then they come out with all these stupid and rather feeble excuses in an attempt to justify what they have done. Such as ah well, if I hadn't shot it someone else would have, which to me still doesn't by any means justify their actions.

This is the best one though. On the other hand, if I hadn't shot it then it probably would have starved to death anyway.

Well sorry mate but I hate to tell you this, but you can't save a species by killing it. Furthermore, they appear to have got the hang of catching their food a very long time ago; and please believe me when I say they don't get to grow that big by starving.

Now there's an ever increasing number of people out there that care a great deal about what's happening to the animals and the world in general, and the first person that springs to mind is of course Sir David Attenborough. Now there's a knighthood that was both well-earned and greatly deserved. So much respect, and indeed gratitude goes out to that man, because without the knowledge I've learned over the years from his and other similar programmes, I very much doubt if this book would have ever been written.

Now you think of all the many different animals, plants and even entire forests that this man has seen that will never be seen by another pair of eyes ever again, simply because thanks to humanity's greed, they no longer exist. Which I find very sad, disgusting, and furthermore extremely embarrassing for our highly evolved, and super intelligent species to say the least I wonder how humanity would react if it was the other way around, and some creature was doing it's best to destroy our species and the planet. I bet it would be a very different story then. Now Sir David Attenborough has been doing what he does for the past sixty years this year 2012. Yet you can still see the immense pleasure he gets out of doing a job he so obviously enjoys very much, which I think is absolutely brilliant and I genuinely take my hat off to the man.

In addition, of course we have the WWF, Greenpeace, Friends of the earth, the WDC and many other like minded organizations who are also doing their best to get things sorted out and from what I can gather they seem to be doing a very good job of it so far. Because more and more people are now starting to realize that what these Organizations have been saying over and over for so many years in an attempt to get us to listen is in fact true.

And they are now beginning to pay closer attention to what these Organizations have to say, and no longer think of them as nothing more than a bunch of troublesome old Hippies who have nothing better to do.

So please don't underestimate the difference you, your family, and your friends could make just by going on their websites and signing their petitions. And maybe even make a donation, which would be very gratefully received, and it genuinely would make a big difference. It's just such a shame that some of the big companies don't give these organizations the money they so desperately need, and possibly make it tax deductible for the donating company which I think is fair enough because if it acts as an incentive for businesses to make donations then excellent lets do it.

(The government does it) However, I would also like to take this opportunity to thank the people that organize and run the Glastonbury festival, which is in Somerset for the contribution they make each year.

Right then moving on to the next topic, perhaps if the morons who are rapidly bulldozing the rainforest into oblivion managed to borrow a few brain cells from somewhere then maybe between them they just might be able to work out that if they cut the trees down and here's the clincher. Then replanted some more trees that actually belong there Indigenous sustainable forest Instead of these palm oil trees that have replaced them and stretch for as far as the eye can see in all directions and look as if they intend to take over the place, which I believe to be the general idea. Then maybe this "little problem" we are experiencing at the moment might not have been so bad. Or at least given us a little bit more of a breathing space, and extra time to sort things out which I dare say we would have more than probably ignored. Nevertheless, you never know I could be wrong, and I'll probably be told in great detail by at least one knowledgeable person just how wrong I am, which is fair enough, and as I mentioned earlier I would invite them to sit down and discuss it with me. We are all entitled to our opinion and I am just expressing mine.

Right then, I mentioned earlier on about the many organizations out there trying to correct the mistakes we have made. This of course includes the wildlife parks and the zoos, as many of them have been running worldwide captive breeding programmes for several years for many of the creatures they have in their care so fair play and thankyou to them for all the hard work and time they continue to dedicate to it, and also for all their help.

As we, all know the zoos have gone through some fundamental changes over the years, considering what they were like when they opened their doors to the public for the very first time all those years ago. It was just animals kept in cages for people to gawp at, with little knowledge of or no regard for the occupant's welfare and health. However, as I said, thankfully those days are long gone because if it wasn't for the zoo's intervention many of these species would now no longer exist.

So maybe mankind isn't all bad, which to be perfectly honest I really don't believe mankind is. Although you have to admit, there have been some "that's not the best thing to do" moments, and an awful lot of them as well.

Right then here's another one of those sod the consequences stories. There are some very large and very dodgy companies out there who, rather than pay to dispose of the waste products they've produced, some of which are really bad. They decide it makes more sense (and also much cheaper) to shall we say, "Hide them" somewhere out of the way normally in the ground, or the rivers, sometimes in the atmosphere, or indeed all of them, and then of course let's not forget everybody's favourite dumping ground the oceans.

Then you have the strip miners who simply power wash away the soil and whatever else that's holding the minerals, precious stones, or metals their looking for straight into the ground and of course into the watercourses. Along with anything else they don't want including the bad stuff, which they are not particularly worried about, because once again its surplus to requirements.

And they have no concern whatsoever for the local village people who are either dropping like flies because they've gone down with one of our many diseases, or are being born with all sorts of deformities, or the village people start developing all sorts of "mysterious and strange illnesses" which of course are all completely unexplainable. And have absolutely nothing whatsoever to do with what's been going on around them.

Furthermore once the miners have finished they normally just pack up and leave, not bothering to reinstate the land they've demolished. The people who live anywhere near these sites are abandoned, they then realize that any promises given by the miners were never going to be fulfilled. Furthermore, any complaints they make to the authorities or directly to the mining company themselves, are more often than not completely ignored.

Except for the individuals and charitable foundations that do the very best they can to help these unfortunate people. Sadly, as usual these charities are pretty much on their own, very under funded, and understaffed (sound familiar?) Well Like I said we really don't make things easy for ourselves do we. Unfortunately, the people who are responsible for causing these problems in the first place are long gone, never even giving the people whose lives they disrupted so much as a second thought. Now Eighty per cent of these minerals are consumed by only twenty per cent of the population and by the end of this century over mining will have used up practically all of the planets reserves.

Yet they still carry on regardless of the consequences, could it be possible that these people don't even realize they're doing anything wrong? Otherwise, how on earth do they manage to sleep at night? Now that's a scary thought to say the least could it actually be possible to cause so much damage and not even realize it?

God I sincerely hope not. On the other hand, maybe because they do this job all day every day perhaps they've developed a way of just switching off and become blind or immune to the situation? Alternatively, could it be the same as total loss of a memory caused by a bad accident you were involved in, or maybe the truth of the matter is very simply because they really couldn't give a shit.

However, I can't see any of them being a plausible reason except of course for the second one, the total memory loss after a bad accident. Because I personally happen to know quite a few people who have suffered memory loss caused through an accident; all part of the joys of motorcycling I'm sorry to say.

Now then the switching off, and not seeing or realizing what they've done wrong theory may explain a few things, but to be perfectly honest I really don't think it would stand up in a court of law somehow. Although saying that, known murderers have got away with it thanks to a so-called "good solicitor" honestly, the mind boggles at some of the things people are more than willing to do for money. Humanity the intelligent idiot,

Unfortunately, it appears to be the only logical answer because we appear to be rapidly losing our in born survival instinct along with our common sense, plus as our intelligence increases, so does our stupidity, which you would have thought to be an impossible thing to do, simply because one should counteract the other, correct? However as you can see for yourself we are the living proof that this does not happen. Now there's something for the super brains to analyze that should keep them occupied for quite a few years at least. Now I wonder what lucky animal will be selected for that experiment.

Personally, I would recommend using some of the mass murderers, child molesters, terrorists, and rapists that are presently clogging up our judicial system as favourite because they really are surplus to requirements. Furthermore, it would work out a damn sight cheaper than keeping them all warm and cosy in our already overcrowded prisons. Although I suppose that would infringe on their human rights, well first of all they need to qualify as human beings, which as far as I can tell they certainly don't come anywhere near.

Secondly what about the rights of the victims and the victims families, and with that thought in mind, we might as well put them to good use and leave the animals out of the picture altogether, well it makes perfect sense to me. But again, I suspect at least one person will disagree with me, and call me a heartless person for even suggesting such barbaric behaviour.

Oh well I suppose it's all part of life's rich tapestry, it's just such a shame we dropped so many stitches on the way and couldn't be bothered to pick them up, or maybe we didn't realize at the time just how important they would be later on in life. Nevertheless, there is still time to correct and to learn from the mistakes we've made, it's just that to do so now we would have to put our glasses on so that we could see more clearly the mistakes we made, but then that's no hardship really is it?

And most definitely, well worth doing I think, in addition I believe once we've got it all organized and made a start, it wouldn't be as difficult to do as we originally thought, and hopefully the job would become a lot easier to do as we went along.

Now some terrible things have happened because of businesses attempting to cut corners in search of an increase in profit. And here's a prime example and I apologize in advance for bringing up the past.

The Aberfan Disaster Which happened at nine fifteen in the morning on the 21st of October 1966, which was the last day before half term, in a small mining village in the next valley to where I was born and brought up.

The tip (slagheap) Slipped and when it hit the village it destroyed a farm, along with twenty terraced houses, it also buried Pantglas junior school killing one hundred and sixteen children which was near enough an entire generation in one foul swoop, twenty eight adults also lost their lives that day, and many peoples lives were changed forever. And like many people, the memory of that day will stay with me for the rest of my life. (I was twelve years old) the people of Aberfan eventually received a compensation payment from the National Coal Board of five hundred pounds for each child they lost. The N.C.B had been warned beforehand not to put the slagheap where it was because of an underground stream running directly below it.

The N.C.B. however strongly disputed this, and claim they had no idea there was an underground stream running below the slagheap. However, the general public raised and donated £ 1.606.929 (apparently the kray twins donated £100) but the people of Aberfan had to pay £150.000 to have the remains of the slagheap removed. Which to be honest the National Coal Board who owned the slagheap should have without question automatically paid for, even if it was only out of respect for all the people that died that day.

And apparently, the government finally paid the £150.000 back into the disaster fund in 1997; however, if the government had paid the interest that money could have earned then the total paid back would have been roughly two million pounds, therefore after thirty-one years of waiting for repayment the people of Aberfan were still ripped off.

I do apologize to the people of Aberfan for mentioning that terrible day in this book. I know you don't need to be reminded of what happened however, it is very relevant, and is very much what a lot of these big companies are all about, which is of course if they think they can get away with something by cutting corners then they will try their damnedest to do so.

Then of course, we have the natural disasters, such as the hurricanes and tornadoes, which seem to be getting more severe and more frequent.

However, scientist have now come to the conclusion that global warming is indeed a proven result of the intense deforestation programmes being run in the rainforests along with high carbon emissions, as I mentioned earlier the facts speak for themselves.

Then there are the volcanic eruptions, earthquakes, and such like which are of course out of our control, although we are getting better at predicting when and where they will happen however, the rest I'm afraid to say are very much our responsibility. (Referring to pollution and so on) now around about the time I started writing this book (late 2010 ish) there was a meeting of world leaders going on in an attempt to sort out our global warming and associated problems.

And they are already squabbling like little children about how much they are willing to reduce their carbon emissions so they can just barely scrape through by increasing the worlds temperature by just two degrees, which also goes to prove they can be lowered.

However, they have been told in no uncertain terms that it's not low enough, so nothing will be gained, as the world's temperature needs to be decreased not increased. Nevertheless, as usual all the world leaders seem to be interested in is how much money it's going to cost them, and also how the poorer countries are going to need help financially. Which of course the wealthier countries are not even vaguely interested in and claim they can't afford to help, even though they own some of the factories that are causing the pollution in the first place. Because the emission laws in that country are not as strict as they are in others, the labour is cheap and the health and safety regulations are practically non-existent.

As I mentioned earlier there has to be a worldwide emissions limit, and it needs to be strictly enforced. Furthermore, the wealthier countries really can't afford not to help the poorer ones especially when as I mentioned it's mostly the factories owned by them that's creating a lot of the pollution in that country. I bet they can afford new weapons though because the world spends twelve times the amount of money on military expenditure than it does on aid to developing countries, and because of this five thousand people die everyday through having to drink dirty water.

And one billion people don't have clean drinking water. Furthermore, one billion people worldwide are going hungry while over fifty percent of all grain traded around the world is turned into bio fuel, or animal feed. And over forty per cent of all arable land has suffered from long-term damage, while in Australia over half of the farmland has already suffered some major damage thanks to severe droughts, which appear to be getting worse, again all thanks to global warming.

Now fair play to whoever managed to get them all around the table in the first place in an attempt to get our problem solved, now they need to lock the doors, and keep them in there until they all come to a satisfactory agreement, its big stick time I think.

For Christ's sake, these people are supposed to be world leaders, so I would have thought they would have to be intelligent and well-educated people. But then maybe that's where the problem comes from because they obviously live in a completely and very different, world to the one the majority of us live in.

For example, they don't have to worry about where the money to pay the bills is coming from, or whether they have enough money to buy food and clothing for their children. Yet they are still ignoring, and can't see, or understand what's going on around them, even when it's been explained in great detail to them.

Are they just too stupid, naïve, or indeed vain enough to believe that none of what's happening to the planet will have any effect on their lives in any way whatsoever, just because they are temporarily important, or famous.

Well unfortunately for them, importance and fame are both very short lived, as I am fairly certain they will discover for themselves soon enough.

In addition they need to realize that they will die someday just like the rest of us. Because it really doesn't matter if someone's famous and incredibly rich, or a destitute beggar living on the street, global warming will affect each and every one of us in one way or another.

However, the other thing that has somehow been overlooked and definitely needs to be taken into consideration is the fact that whatever the final decision these world leaders arrive at during these political summits, will greatly affect not only their children's but also their grandchildren's lives, either for the better or for the worse. Furthermore, they are the ones that will have to live with whatever decision they make, so the choice boils down to your children's wellbeing, or profit.

Talking of children's wellbeing, did you know that the trade in child slave labour is still thriving and even increasing in some parts of the world?

Now the place I intend to focus on is the Ivory Coast where children as young as seven years old are being sold to slave traders for a few dollars. Because the parents of these young children have been told a pack of lies, such as the children would be well looked after and receive a good education, and how the parents will be very proud of their children's achievements when they return home.

When in fact these children are forced to work really long hours in the cocoa fields and if they don't work hard enough, or they work to slow they receive a merciless beating plus they won't be fed that day, I doubt if they get a lot of food anyway. Now a lot of the cocoa buyers and chocolate manufacturers have become aware of what is happening and have stopped trading with the people that use child slave labour.

Except for one company that despite receiving a petition that had been signed by several thousands of people (which includes myself) yet they are still refusing to stop using child labour. Now this is a big company who unfortunately, I can't name for legal reasons however, I know that the filmmakers who were using this well known company to produce its promotional chocolate have now been told about the child slave labour that's being used to harvest the cocoa beans. so I can't really see the contract being renewed unless they change their ways.

I know I keep saying this, but we really could quite easily make life so much better for ourselves and maybe even begin to enjoy being alive once more, and not have to worry about the condition of the world, or what's happening to it. This would make myself and quite a few other people a damn sight happier for a start.

Some people believe it's nice to have a dream, and they are quite right, unfortunately, the only thing that's stopping this dream from becoming a reality is ourselves.

Therefore, the next question is just how long do we have to keep saying these things need to be put right before anyone in authority pays any attention? Because they need to start getting things organized, and do something about solving these problems.

Now at the time of writing this book, the WWF and the SKY TV people have joined forces and are asking

The Entelligent Idiot

people for donations to help buy parts of the rain forest, and SKY have promised to match each donation received. Therefore, for example if someone donates ten pounds or ten thousand pounds, SKY would also donate the same amount, and fair play to them.

They will accept any amount as a donation, three pounds a month would help to buy and maintain an acre of rain forest and it really would make a huge difference, so please visit their website. www.wwf.org.uk/skyrainforest rescue to find out how you could help, in addition, a very big thankyou to them for taking the initiative and for getting the ball rolling, now do you believe for one minute that our illustrious world leaders will take a blind bit of notice? Or maybe even take advantage of this very generous offer to help save the rainforests, no? And strangely enough neither do I. I doubt if they even know what these people are trying to do, and even if they did would they care?

Unfortunately, I really don't think the majority of them would. However, I would be most grateful if they would prove me wrong, but with actions, not empty meaningless words and broken promises.

Now as I mentioned earlier about big companies, which basically is what our world governments are. And how they have a very bad habit of leaving things to us the "general public" to sort out, while they sit back making all sorts of ridiculous reassuring noises, but as usual doing absolutely nothing at all to help.

Which makes me wonder just what exactly; these laughably called world leaders do for us? Apart from lining their pockets, and fiddling the system, and therefore us the taxpayer, by claiming for second mortgages, bath plugs, porno films and one member of parliament even tried to claim for having his moat cleaned on so-called expenses. It's legally okay for them to make these claims, but only because they passed the laws to make it so. However, I personally along with a lot of other people believe it to be morally wrong.

Especially when they get caught trying to "fiddle" even more money on their expense accounts than their entitled to when most of them already have more money in the bank than we the "common working man" will ever see or earn in our entire lifetime. Most British politicians earn between £187.000 and £200.000 a year and that's not including expenses or the three hundred pound tax-free payments they get for each time they show up in parliament. If we attempted to fiddle money out of our place of work we would be done for fraud yet the politicians just get told off and they may be made to pay it back whereas we would be prosecuted and more than likely end up in prison so there's one law for them and one for us.

On September 13th 2013, it was reported in the newspapers that this year our illustrious "we are all in this together" members of parliament have claimed the highest ever recorded sum of ninety eight million pounds in expenses, now you have to admit that this is just pure greed, I mean its not as if they need the extra money. And if that's not bad enough, on top of that, one hundred and fifty five MPs also used some of our hard earned tax money to put a few of their relatives on the payroll.

Just think of the things that could have been used for, because that is a hell of a lot of wasted money. And just to rub salt into the wound these politicians are still getting away with it, some with their over sea's bank accounts. Therefore, they don't legally have to pay much if any tax in this country.

And now they have the nerve to complain about and condemn the big foreign companies to which they granted permission allowing them to operate in this country for doing exactly the same thing as they are.

So it would appear the majority of these politicians are nothing more than greedy, money grabbing hypocrites, yet we still allow them to run our country.

And now the government are reducing the heating allowances and other benefits for the elderly and disabled (including the people that became disabled through defending their country) these people rely heavily on these payments especially during the winter months, but the government say we have no other choice and we need to make these cut backs. And they make these ludicrous "we are all in this together" speeches which are obviously complete and utter nonsense because as usual we are the ones struggling to keep warm and to feed ourselves, while they continue to rob us blind.

And they keep on about how there's no money in the coffers and that's the reason for all of these cutbacks, yet their lives haven't changed in the slightest, if anything to be honest thanks to the record expenses claims, I dare say their lifestyle has improved no end.

(It would also help to explain why we don't have any money in the coffers) but not only are they ripping us off they are also insulting our intelligence, because after all the we'll struggle through this crisis together speeches.

It has now come to light that they now intend to give themselves an 11 percent pay rise in the not too distant future and they say the pay rise is out of their hands and they have no say in the matter. However, the best thing is they say that they can't legally refuse to accept this big pay rise, and I bet that really upsets them. Even if it's true and they cant refuse the wage increase there's nothing to stop them donating it to charity. Because they still keep saying we all have to make these cutbacks in order to get this country back on its feet, while we the general public are supposed to sit back and suffer in silence. I think when a politician say's "we" they obviously mean us the "common man." For example, the public are suffering and there are food banks opening up all over the country because many people can no longer afford to buy food. Then you have people who at their wits end are committing suicide because they can't afford to pay the new "bedroom tax" that was recently introduced by the government, now what I struggle to understand is how can they tax you for a bedroom your already paying for in your council tax?

Then, while all of this is going on, it's reported in the newspapers that one Member of Parliament who obviously lives in his own little world completely oblivious to what's going on in the rest of the country. Suddenly decides to apply for planning permission to build a bloody big indoor swimming pool in the grounds of one of his houses.

So can you really say with conviction that we are not the intelligent idiots? And if you believe, you can. Then you have just proven my point. And I'm sorry but I disagree with you, and I bet I can say that with a damn sight more conviction than some people because the truth is staring us straight in the face if we only bothered to look.

However, like I said please prove me wrong, but with deed's, not empty promises.

Now I don't class myself as an intelligent person by any means, and if I appear to come across as a know it all then I really do apologize as it's not intentional, because I really am as common as sheep shit on a welsh hillside,

And I am a very down to earth sort of person.

But as far as I'm concerned, everything I have written here to the best of my knowledge is true. In addition, common sense and having your eyes and ears open will prove its right. And as the legendary Bob Dylan once said in a song, you don't need to be a weatherman to know which way the wind blows.

Now earlier on I mentioned Sir David Attenborough and how long he's been doing what he does, and once again I say fair play to the man, now I have also discovered thanks to him that during those sixty years Humanity has tripled in number, and that every eleven years the world's population increases by one billion.

I have also discovered that some of the big banks are now paying beef farmers in Brazil to allow some of their land to be used for the replanting of trees. Now this in my eyes is a good thing.

Except for the fact that the banks are then selling the farmers carbon credits to the big conglomerates, to make their carbon footprint appear lower than they really are. Which, apparently these banks can legally do? Although as far as I'm concerned, it's nothing more than a con.

But then on a more positive note at least we get more natural rainforest being planted, instead of palm oil plantations, which has to be a plus.

Unfortunately, once again what I struggle to understand, is why as usual these businesses are going the long way around things? Because surely it would make more sense for these big conglomerates to just pay for replanting the trees themselves or better still just donate the money they pay to the banks directly to the WWF/SKY venture. Which would instantly double the amount donated and it would also put these big firms in a much better light with an awful lot of people who would be thinking well at least their doing something, and trying to help. It's also a very good advertising strategy.

In addition, I would have thought it would work out more cost effective especially if they donated it because I can't really see these banks going through all that trouble to set this up for nothing. Out of the goodness of their hearts or from their love for humanity somehow can you? Which brings me back to what I mentioned earlier, about the top brains usually finding the hardest or most awkward way of doing things and being paid thousands of pounds for doing so.

I mean all these big companies have to do is to get some office junior with a bit of common sense, to look through the phone book, or most probably the internet, and look under rancher, then phone or email the person, offer him or her a deal and its job done.

On the other hand, as I mentioned the really easy option is to ring or email the WWF/SKY venture at, sky rainforest rescue wwf.org or www.wwf.uk/skyrainforest rescue, and they will quite happily do the rest. In addition, as I mentioned earlier maybe the company making the donation could get it deducted from their tax bill.

Which is fair enough I think, not hard to do really is it? All you have to do is pick up the phone, or visit their website. Perhaps I should apply for a job as a top brain I'm certainly thick enough.

Nevertheless, to be absolutely honest, I believe I would still be over qualified, because I still have common sense, logic, and a very strong survival instinct all of which I believe you need to have surgically removed before you can qualify as a top brain. Because these are really intelligent people (on paper) however, in reality they appear to have very little or no common sense Therefore, I don't think I'll bother really.

And to be honest I don't think I could cope with some jumped up little jobs worth dictating what I can and can't do. Plus all that jargon and red tape diplomacy malarkey,

I think I would end up punching someone, so that's no good then is it, ah, well never mind.

Then we have the local council's setting up all these recycling schemes, and fair play to them at least their trying to help. On the other hand, maybe I should say some of them want you to believe they're trying to help, let me give you an example if I may. One council decided to put three big green recycling bins in every cemetery in its parish, which is fine, and a good idea.

Now have a little think for one moment about what most people take with them when they visit their loved ones in the cemetery.

Personally, I would take flowers, which are normally wrapped in some sort of plastic or cellophane, I would also take a plastic bottle full of water to pour on them, once I have placed them in the vase on the grave, (once I've removed the old dead flowers) makes sense yes.

So now I've got a handful of dead flowers and plastic to get rid of, right then so it's off to the recycling bins I go and that's it job done right? Wrong, because written on these recycling bins it states in big letters that no vegetation or plastic of any kind is to be placed in these bins.

Honestly, and right next to these empty bins, there was a small mountain of rotting flowers and plastic which to be honest didn't smell very healthy to say the least.

And when the person in charge of maintaining the cemetery was asked what was the point of putting the recycling bins there if no one could use them his reply was, at least we look as if we are trying to help, oh right, not to stupid then? However, if you have recycling bins outside your home then God only help you if purely by accident something gets placed in the wrong bin. Because for some unknown reason.

It creates complete and utter chaos for the people emptying them not to mention a nasty fine for you to pay, then what does the government do to recycle all of this waste you've so carefully sifted through. Do they recycle all the plastic, paper, and aluminium cans, apparently, yes, most of them do, but the bulk of it is shipped abroad to a place called Gambia. Honestly, talk about not in my back yard, now this rubbish includes everything from babies' dirty nappies to televisions and computers, and I bet the shipping costs don't come cheaply.

Now there are firms in this country that recycle old plastic, by turning it into insulation products for your loft and stud walling etc, which apparently is safer and cleaner to use than the insulation that's made using fibreglass. (No nasty itchiness) so why don't the local councils recycling chappie's get off their arses, and go and talk to these people and come up with some mutually beneficial plan? In addition, if they sold this insulation at a sensible price, then everyone would be happy.

Unlike some of these daft idea's they come up with to look as if they're trying to do their job. Oh yes the councils actually employ people to deal with recycling and alternative methods of disposal. Well, some of them are definitely not worth employing. Maybe they should recycle their wages, or maybe a trip to the jobcentre would be a good idea for some of them.

Now we all know that the local councils are given a certain amount of money (budget) to spend each year and of course they should work out in order of priority how much and where this money should be spent, makes perfect sense to me. Except for one thing, if the councils have to get rid of any surplus money before the end of the tax year, at least spend it on something useful instead of wasting it. And I'm certain this goes on all over the country, and more than probably all over the world.

Furthermore, I bet if you added up all the money these people squandered every year it would come to quite a substantial amount, which of course could and most definitely should, be used on much better and certainly more important matters. Such as solar panels, wind and / or water turbines, and anything else that would help the planet recover. I know I keep saying this, but I genuinely cannot work these people out. Now I know there are many people out there that feel just as strongly as I do on this matter, and I sincerely hope that the majority of you will agree with some, if not all that I've written here.

Right then, now we have all seen these adverts on the television, the radio and in the newspapers telling us not to leave our televisions, computers, play stations, Xboxes, etc on standby. And how we all need to drive at least five miles less a week to help reduce our carbon emissions, fine and if everybody done so, it would probably help to make a difference.

However, has anyone in authority bothered to tell these big companies that spew out millions of tonnes of the stuff each and every year that they need to reduce their emissions? Probably yes, they have. Nevertheless, I very much doubt if quite a few of the firms producing these gases have tried very hard to find a solution to the problem. Alternatively, they make a token attempt just to "show willing" but not really achieving anything.

Also the fines they receive for not complying might appear to be a lot of money to you and me. But to them it's just petty cash, and I dare say it probably works out cheaper to pay the fines, than to upgrade and fit new improved filter system's and so on.

These firms need to be told firmly, clearly, and precisely how in the future they will be given a strict time limit to have the work and improvements done by, or the factory will be completely shut down except for maintenance work until all the improvements are completed.

However, these emission limits need to be global, in other words these limits are to be applied worldwide. Because it would stop these companies closing down their factories in this and other countries with similar emission limits to ours and relocating the entire workload to another country where the labour is cheap, plus the health and safety, along with the emission limits are not so strict. That should get their attention. Because it would effectively close the "back door" so they really wouldn't have much choice and would have to get the work done however, if they don't get the improvements done within the set time limit and try to bluff their way out of it then shut them down.

I think it's time to get tough with these companies and when they say if you shut us down then all of our workforce will be made unemployed then I would call their bluff. Because these companies would not want to be closed, furthermore, if they can't relocate because of a global emissions limit, they would have no choice in the matter therefore, no one would be unemployed for long if at all. These companies need to be taken by the scruff of the neck and given a very thorough shaking, no more Mr nice person. The same standards should also be applied to our illustrious world leaders.

Because they also need to be told in no uncertain terms that they can no longer get away with their "tall stories" and to stop all the bullshitting, and scheming. And we should also give them a realistic time limit in which to get the carbon emissions lowered, and by what amount. And if they don't get it done, or if they say it would cost too much money to get these things changed, or whatever other excuses they dream up, then don't mess about just sack them by using a vote of no confidence.

Because they're there to serve us and to do what they're told, and not vice versa as they appear to think, my next question to them would be is it actually possible to put a price on being able to watch your children growing up in a better, cleaner, and safer world.

Not to mention saving the entire planet and all of its inhabitant's so what it really comes down to then, is good old fashioned common sense doesn't it? Because it really is a no brainer, Oh, and one other important thing to remember is, we really don't have any choice in the matter we all know it needs to be done immediately. Now we have had the technology and the capability to do it for many years, so let's get on and do it.

As I mentioned earlier we are more than capable of doing the job, the hardest part is getting our world governments, and the big businesses that are responsible for most of the pollution interested enough to give a shit. I recommend the get it done or sack them approach.

Or in the case of the big businesses we just need to stop buying all of their products in order to get their attention, and if they still refuse to change then we should continue to boycott them until we eventually bankrupt them.

Because despite what these big companies believe, they need us the general money spending public, a damn sight more than we will ever need them, because we can survive quite happily without any of their products (despite what the advertising media try to tell us) however, they on the other hand cannot survive without us. So in a nutshell, the only thing stopping us from solving our global warming and associated problems is us.

Now just how stupid does this sound? Imagine you are sat in the pub and a friend comes up and tells you that another planet the same as ours has just been discovered. However, the so-called most intelligent animal on that planet doesn't have enough sense, or are just too stupid, to stop themselves from destroying the very thing they need to survive (the planet) And therefore themselves, and everything else that lives there with them, honestly, what would you think, Idiots? I rest my case.

The same thing applies to our public transport systems, the conditions on them appear to be getting lower and lower, and the fares are climbing higher and higher. Maybe if the transport companies spent more of their huge profits on modernising and updating the systems and making it a more reliable method of transport instead of giving themselves these ridiculously high bonuses. And maybe even lowered the fares, or at least made it value for money then I dare say a lot more people would be willing to use them because they want to, instead of using them because they have no other choice and have to use them. However, these companies seem to think if their profits are not massively increased each year then they must be running at a loss.

Now if you're above breaking even, and therefore making money then surely a profit is a profit, whichever way you look at it correct? Now I know all businesses are there to make a profit and that's fine. Unfortunately, some of these companies appear to be getting somewhat complacent, and shall we say a little bit on the greedy side because as far as they're concerned they've cornered the market, because some people have no other option and they have to use the services (no matter how poor) these companies provide.

So the passengers will just have to put up with the conditions and why should the highly paid bosses worry about it because there's no way you would catch them using public transport, unless of course its for some sort of promotional scheme to justify another fare increase.

Nevertheless, as usual it's us the general public that suffer the consequences. Maybe if, as I said the bosses stopped giving themselves these ridiculously high bonuses each year, then things might look a bit better for them. Unfortunately, I can't see that happening anytime soon somehow can you, simply because as I mentioned earlier, man is by nature a greedy animal.

Now did you know that China and Australia are among the biggest producers and users of coal with India coming in just behind them, therefore you can just imagine the amount of greenhouse gases they produce every year. Although in all fairness to Australia, because apparently the countries largest power company are now talking about using captured carbon emissions from one of its coal fired plants to help grow algae that will then be processed into clean transport fuel. So let's hope they eventually do the same to all the coal fired plants.

Furthermore, let's hope China and India follow in their footsteps, or even better make it a worldwide law so all coal-fired plant have to be fitted with the same equipment then there would be no need to drill for oil.

Did you know it would take three million years to produce just one year's supply of coal for one of these countries to use, and the same rule applies to oil production. Therefore, we really do need to find and start using the alternative "new technology" and the sooner the better, because as we all know the planet doesn't have as we once thought limitless reserves of coal, gas, and oil and they are now rapidly running out and it's also getting more and more difficult to extract.

This means we really don't have any choice in the matter so using this "new technology" has to be done.

Now speaking of oil, did you know that in 2007, a massive oil field was discovered beneath the ocean in Ghana? And they named it the jubilee field, this oil was discovered by a firm that goes by the name of Kosmos, but the Ghana national Petroleum Corporation (or GNPC for short) runs Ghana's oil industry Furthermore, the Ghanaian government owns GNPC; also, GNPC is one of Kosmos' partners in the jubilee field.

Nigeria is one of the largest exporters of oil in Africa, and the fifth largest supplier to the United States. Nevertheless, unfortunately life for the average Nigerian has become much worse since this oil was first discovered there over fifty years ago. Because between 1960 and 1999 Nigerian officials have either stolen or squandered a grand total of 44 billion dollars, this country is consistently ranked as one of the most corrupt in the world.

Most of the stolen money comes from oil exports, and most of this oil comes from the Niger delta, which is Nigeria's main oil producing region.

However, apparently steps are now being taken to stop the corruption and they also intend to shut down the firms that deal with these corrupt officials. Now since the winter of 2005 militant groups have been sabotaging pipelines in Nigeria, therefore shutting down massive amounts of oil production.

Now the reason for the sabotage is the people are demanding for much more of the profit to be shared with the people who live in the Niger delta, which I personally think is only fair. There is a militant group called the deadly underdogs who claim one top government official alone embezzled 250 million dollars.

Yet a lot of people are still living in slums and hovels all across the country. And they are calling the oil field a "resource curse" because of its similarity to their gold mining rights being exploited for hundreds of years yet the people that live there have absolutely nothing whatsoever to show for it.

Therefore, the people are now quite rightly complaining about the foreign companies coming to their country simply to exploit their resources, and the people are now angry because they are not benefiting from these resources. In addition, they want a say in how the money should be spent, for example education, and improving people's lives, including healthcare, stamping out poverty and starvation, and also one of their major problems is not having clean water to drink. Because the money oil will bring into their country is a phenomenal amount. Now the newly elected president has promised to spend the majority of this money on improving the country and the lives of its people. The new president has also arranged a meeting with the oil producers to discuss the new terms of contract.

Now in Nigeria there is a very strong illegal trade in something called condensate fuel. Which is in fact a low-grade petrol that is being sold illegally through the backdoors of various oil companies refineries. It has also become a main source of income for many of the local people, and they are quite blatant about it, and can be seen quite openly transporting it in various ways through the main streets of the towns and villages.

However, because this is a highly flammable liquid combined with the fact that many of these people quite frequently transport it in unsealed containers, would help to explain why there have been numerous cases of people being burnt, and some people have died of their injuries. Nevertheless, they seem to see it as an acceptable risk and business in this illegal trade is thriving, even though its highly volatile, many people are still quite willing to buy it simply because it's so cheap.

It has also been discovered that certain firms are paying the local people to cut through the main oil pipelines and then set fire to them so these firms can get the clean-up contracts. However, some people are cutting into these pipelines and stealing the oil to sell, then as usual you have a few people that become greedy because some wealthy Gambians are going to extremes. Because they have tapped into the main distribution pipeline and are pumping this oil into big barges and then transferring it into the oil tankers that are waiting anchored just off shore, and these already wealthy people are making billions of pounds from this illegal trade. Once again, the government is doing its best to stop it.

The government has also negotiated a new contract with the firms responsible for extracting the oil officially. Now in the first year of production the foreign companies have made more than two billion dollars from the oil, and Ghana received forty-one million dollars nevertheless, just how much of this money the people of Ghana will receive remains to be seen.

Now in Canada they have started extracting the oil from the tar sands. And the biggest Lorries in the world move thousands of tons of this sand on a daily basis.

However, the process of heating the sand to separate it from the bitumen, millions of cubic metres of water and huge amounts of energy are used, and the pollution that's created by this process is catastrophic. However, as I said earlier these companies have no intention of stopping until they have bled this planet dry as our resources become smaller and smaller and our demands for energy gets higher and higher.

And we have now reached the point of no return where the planet can no longer cope with our demands, at the moment we would need a planet one and a half times bigger than the earth. Yet like a spoilt child we still continue to stamp our feet and throw tantrums as we defiantly demand more and more not caring in the slightest about how we get it, at what cost, or where it comes from, just as long as we get it.

On the news, I caught the tail end of a report about someone who has suggested bringing in a bank and stock exchange tax. Apparently, this would be a very small amount something like 000.5 per cent.

Nevertheless, the beauty of this tiny little tax is it would raise approximately four hundred and fifty thousand pounds every year. Which would then be used to help the poorer countries get on their feet, which I think is a brilliant idea. Another use would be in the fight against global warming, and also help towards saving the many highly endangered plant and wildlife species, which is an excellent idea I just hope they bring it into force, and the sooner the better really. I can't wait for the outcome of this one, although I dare say the most likely thing to happen will be it just disappears without a trace never to be seen or heard of again.

I bet many of the big companies will be against it for whatever desperate reasons they can think of, most of which will be the usual pathetic little "whining" noises such as you can't do it because my mummy said you're not allowed to, sort of thing. However, if by some miracle it is passed and becomes law then yippee as there would be no legitimate reason (which, of course there isn't anyway,) for stopping people getting on with things. Although I can practically guarantee some slimy little government officials, will try their utmost to get their sweaty little hands on this new fund.

Because in their eyes that is an awful lot of money just begging to be spent and what sort of idiot would want to waste all that lovely money on something as trivial as saving the planet.

Nevertheless, I must admit we would need someone who knows what they're doing in charge of this fund. Now personally, I would recommend making someone like Greenpeace, Friends of the earth and the WWF administrators. Because, they already have the organization, along with the expertise, and the contacts furthermore, they are already doing a brilliant job helping to save the rainforest, animals, the oceans and of course the global warming problem of this planet.

Plus they already know exactly what the job entails. Therefore, no super brains need apply that should save several thousands of pounds straight away, nevertheless as I said you can practically guarantee the government will try their best to setup a "special committee" to organize, and run this fund. (And cream vast amounts of money off it in administration charges, bonuses, etc) like I said that is an awful lot of money to waste on saving the world. However, as I said, there's absolutely no need for any special committees just put the people who know what they are doing in charge and your halfway there.

There could be renewable forests for the timber industries, which would help increase the oxygen levels, and all the profits would go back into the fund.

The poorer countries would get the help they so desperately need to get them on their feet, and have a decent education. Most if not all of the energy needs could be met by renewable means such as solar panels, wind and water turbines because you would practically be starting with a blank canvas.

I don't mean any offence by this statement mind but because they don't have anything at the moment therefore, if we intend to change the world for the better

The Entelligent Idiot

then this would be an ideal place to start, and also an ideal opportunity to show the world that it can be done.

Then all the other countries would realise that it is quite possible to survive, and even flourish without the use of any fossil fuels, because using them is literally costing us the earth.

Then of course, once people see how much cleaner and fresher everything is, then I dare say they would also want to change to these alternative means of producing energy. And once that happens, then more and more people would start demanding the same, (the snowball effect) then I'm glad to say there wouldn't be a single government in the world that could stop it happening.

Now that really would be something to see, (hopefully in my lifetime) now I must admit none of these changes are going to happen overnight. Nevertheless, once you have an entire country whose energy needs are virtually met by using only renewable and free resources, then that would change from a very poor country to a very rich one in many ways because that country would then become the building block for the rest of the world to follow. Which I believe would happen very quickly and the demand for this "alternative energy resource" would soar, simply because of mankind's constant need for the latest technology and gadgets. Along with the well if they've got one then I want one too sort of attitude (or as we like to call it keeping up with the joneses) now I know once it's all in place and working properly it will all need to be maintained.

Nevertheless this has to be cheaper, cleaner, easier, and definitely safer to work on than a nuclear reactor surely? Then of course, we have the battery and hydrogen cell cars to consider, because once they are in full production then the manufacturers would continue to improve on them, and they would become a lot cheaper to produce, buy, and to run. I mean just look at the very first cars ever produced, for example the model T ford. If you were to compare them to what we drive around in today then they are worlds apart, yet the basic principal is exactly the same.

However let's go back to that bank tax I mentioned earlier. Can you imagine all the things we could do with this fund if it did become official? With little, or preferably no intervention whatsoever from any government's, and should be registered as a charitable institution therefore, the government would not be able to tax it, or claim any part of it for political use.

Which should upset quite a few top officials because they won't be able to get their sweaty little hands on any of it, I recommend they put a few of their top brains on it that should make certain they never get anything at all, that should wipe them smarmy little smirk's off their faces. Now please don't get me wrong, I'm not anti-government by any means.

It's just that I can't tolerate bullshitter's, liars, and schemer's (oh, well in that case maybe I am then) anyway let's get back to this fund; I've just realized how crucial it is to get it passed as law. Because if it is then we could get on with the job almost immediately within reason, and red tape allowing, unfortunately, if it's not made law then it's back to square one.

Which is trying to persuade and convince the world governments to get motivated enough to stop talking about our problems and do something about them.

Then on the other hand, we might just get lucky and this small tax will meet with no opposition whatsoever, and will fly straight through to law. However I won't be holding my breath.

Two years have now passed since I started writing this book. And unfortunately, I was right about the bank tax, because it appears to have vanished off the face of the earth with nothing more being mentioned, or written about it. Which I think, is so sad because we could have done so much with that money.

And because it was going to be such a small tax, I doubt if anyone would have objected or even noticed they were paying it. However, I can't find any information about it anywhere, so it appears someone nipped this one in the bud very early on in the game, sour grapes maybe.

Anyway moving on, earlier I mentioned all these adverts on the television, and in the newspapers telling people to drive five miles less per week to help the environment, and of course, it would certainly help.

So once again, I am somewhat confused as to why they keep asking people to do these things, and then on the other hand they continue to build these massive shopping centres in the middle of nowhere? So unfortunately, you don't really have much of a choice, because you have to drive (usually up some motorway) to get to these shopping centres. Maybe these government people need to sit down and try talking to each other every now and again. Now please don't try to tell me these shopping centres help to ease the traffic in the towns and villages, because it doesn't. Because you normally have to drive through these towns and villages, to get to the motorway, to get to these shopping centres anyway.

In addition, I dare say we have all wasted several hours sat in traffic jams on the motorway, especially on a bank holiday weekend, whilst attempting to get either to or from these places, correct?

Also thanks to these big shopping centres, the small local shops and builders merchants in these towns and villages are having their prices drastically undercut by these superstores. And because of this, and the resulting loss of customers they are forced to close down, then of course, you get the local residents complaining about the closure of their local shops.

Even though they are inadvertently responsible for their closure in the first place, well personally, I much prefer to use the local shops, okay you may have to pay a small amount more for your goods. However, if you actually sat down and worked it out, in most cases it would work out cheaper. Because that little bit extra you paid for your goods would not only save you time, and more than likely cover the cost of the fuel you would have used driving to these big superstores.

In addition, no traffic jams to worry about (because their all stuck on the motorway) furthermore, I know from personal experience that the service given in the local shops and builders merchants is first class, and the advice is also given quite freely.

Plus there's normally a much nicer, and friendlier atmosphere in these places, and they don't seem to be in any particular rush to get you through the till. And they have made many jobs I have done so much easier.

Right then, just for a moment let's go back to these decision makers not talking to each other as it's pretty much the same story with the electricity. Once again, we have all these adverts on the television, radio, or in the newspapers, telling us not to leave our play stations, televisions and whatever else on standby. And how we should remove the plugs from their electrical sockets to save energy, fine, it makes perfect sense to me.

However, the next time you go to the shop or supermarket to do your shopping have a quick look around while your in there, and see just how many air fresheners there are that have to be plugged into an electrical socket just to get the damn things to work.

Which to me seems to override the energy saving suggestion somehow?

Now how, did we ever manage before some clown came up with this idea as a "new angle of approach" which would then be used as an advertising gimmick or as they prefer to call it an advertising "strategy" to make people believe the plug in versions work so much better than any "normal" air freshener would? Yet in the past people never had to plug freshly cut flowers into anything to enjoy their fragrance, And you most certainly don't need to plug dog shit into anything to know that it's there; if you know what I mean, so with a little bit of media manipulation people will believe near enough anything the adverts tell them. And once again it just goes to prove just how gullible so many people are.

Right then, now let's talk about the palm oil that's being illegally grown and harvested in Indonesia. I bet you never knew that palm oil is in a surprisingly wide variety of things that we use every day, which includes lipstick, and the soap you wash with, also the toothpaste you use to clean your teeth. To the breadcrumbs on your favourite fish fingers, along with so many other things that if I wrote them all down it would be another book. And a staggering eighty per cent of all palm oil grown and harvested in Indonesia is done so illegally.

And in order to keep up with the ever-increasing worldwide demand for palm oil, the illegal growers have now started cutting down huge areas of rainforest, most of which are classed as high conservation areas, which were of course created with the intention of protecting the creatures that live there, especially the poor old and very much maligned Orang Utan's.

Now these lovely creatures only breed every eight years, and apparently they have the longest childhood in the animal kingdom, except of course for mankind.

Now their homes are being destroyed at an alarming rate so as usual, the homeless, deeply traumatized, and normally orphaned young Orang Utan's are then looked after by the local charitably run rescue organizations. (Sounds familiar does it?) Unfortunately, the Orang Utan's don't cope at all well with stress, and they are in one hell of a mess when they first arrive at these charitable sanctuaries, this of course is perfectly understandable. Just imagine what you would be like if as a small child you had witnessed your family being slaughtered, simply because they couldn't get out of the tree that was being cut down quickly enough. Then you're left all alone and confused, surrounded by your dead family with no home, nowhere to go, and nothing to eat.

However, in Borneo there's a charity called the Borneo Orang Utan survival foundation that have been rehabilitating these young Orang Utan's in how to live in the wild. First of all they rear them for three years, and then once they are more confident and settled, they select a few to be put on an island where they stay for about eight years.

Now although the Orang Utan's are still getting fed on a daily basis they are also encouraged to find their own food just as they would in the wild.

Well now after ten years of planning, the foundation intend to release some of these Orang Utan's back into the rainforest, the now adult Orang Utan's have been at the foundation since they were first brought there as deeply traumatised babies because their parents had been killed. One young female arrived with four fingers missing off her right hand; they had been cut off with the machete the loggers used to hack her mother to death while she was still clinging to her, and she was then just left there to die. Therefore, her future at first didn't look very promising to say the least, however she surprised everyone by showing them just how clever, determined and highly adaptable she was.

At the moment there are over six hundred orphans at this foundation and their numbers are steadily rising, hopefully all of which will one day also be released back into the wild. However, the foundation initially intend to release six first of all, which consists of three females with babies, and three males to see how they get on, each individual has been fitted with a tracker so they know where they are so the "carers" can keep an eye on them in case of any problems.

Now over the last twenty years Indonesia and Borneo have lost a huge area of rainforest to logging and palm oil plantations, so finding somewhere safe to release the Orang Utan's was a difficult job. So the Orang Utan's ended up being put into cages, then placed on the back of a lorry then onto an aeroplane, and finally being dangled on a steel rope from a helicopter, all of which they appeared to take in their stride with no problems.

Then when they did eventually reach the part of the forest that was going to be their new home the Orang Utan's seemed to settle in within a few hours, and after a couple of weeks they were all eating okay, and appeared to be quite happy and settled in their new surroundings.

So now the organisation had proof that orphaned Orang Utan's are quite capable of living in the wild once they have been taught how to survive.

And another fifteen have recently been released into the same area of forest, they also intend to release another forty-nine by the end of the year which means there will be a brand new colony of Orang Utan's living safely where they belong in the rainforest for many years to come, which I think is really good news.

And fair play to the Borneo Orang Utan survival foundation for all their hard work, perseverance, and the determination to make this dream come true. It's just a shame they have had to do all of this because of the logging companies and the palm oil plantations blind determination to destroy the forest in the name of profit, whilst trying their utmost to convince everyone that they have only our best interests at heart.

Now a mere twenty years ago Borneo which is the fourth largest island on the planet was covered by a huge primary forest, however if they continue with deforestation at the same rate as they are today, it will all be completely destroyed within the next ten years. All thanks to humanity's constant demand for more palm oil, the illegal palm oil producer's make on average five million pounds each year, so it's big business.

Now quite a few journalists have tried many times over the years to investigate this illegal palm oil growing, and they have all been promptly deported for their trouble, so obviously, someone has something to hide.

Now fair play to the people who are in charge of the rainforest conservation, because they are doing their very best to stay on top of this problem however, you can just imagine the vast area's these people have to patrol and protect, and I expect they are very much under funded and understaffed. (This all sounds so familiar) I sincerely hope they receive the funding and all the help they deserve in the not too distant future, because in a mere forty years the Amazon has been reduced by twenty per cent, now a fair bit of this land is then used for cattle ranches.

However, many of these ranches are nothing more than glorified and much bigger versions of our very own battery hen farms. Because the cattle are kept in outside pens, and they never so much as see a blade of grass let alone eat any, because the ground in these pens are nothing more than dust which is created by the constant pounding it receives from the cattle's hooves and these "ranches" are huge.

The land is also used for huge Soya bean plantations, and ninety five per cent of these Soya beans are used to feed poultry and livestock all over Europe and Asia.

Now these illegal growers are also contributing to global warming, not just because they are cutting down the rainforest although that obviously doesn't help.

And of course this also includes the illegal palm oil growers, because if there are three metres or more peat in the ground where they intend to put these plantations then they can't legally disturb it, so by law they can't plant anything there. Because if you disturb the peat it releases carbon monoxide into the atmosphere, two hundred and fifty tons of it each year to be precise which obviously is not a good thing.

However, because the majority of these plantations are illegal then they're obviously not going to be too concerned about illegally digging up the peat.

Fortunately, there does appear to be a light at the end of the tunnel, because now the big palm oil buyers have been informed of this problem and thankfully, the vast majority of them have now cancelled many of the contracts they had with these rogue plantation owners.

And are now adamantly refusing to deal with any, and all palm oil growers that can't legally prove that all of it's products have come from an established and renewable source. Therefore, this should stop, or at least slow down these cowboy growers for a while or at least until they find a way around it, and believe me they will, because that's an awful lot of money to lose over something they'll just class as a trivial legal technicality.

And I dare say there will be some government officials sat in an office somewhere rubbing their hands together thinking about all the money they'll made "sorting" this little legal problem out for them.

However, I would like to say fair play and thankyou to the palm oil buyers for getting involved. All they need to do is remember the names of the managing directors of these suspect firms and use them to cross reference the "new" established companies that will start popping up and let's hope all the other big buyers follow their example and also refuse to buy from known rogue growers. Because thanks to these illegal growers, more than forty per cent of the Orang Utan's habitat have been torn down and needlessly destroyed in the last ten years alone. Now that is an incredible amount and as I said earlier, the equivalent of three full size football pitches of rainforest are cut down, and lost every minute.

Apparently in some parts of the rainforest the soil isn't as fertile as originally thought therefore, it would take many years for the rainforest to grow back naturally and the trees would be a lot smaller, and also a lot weaker, that is of course if they were ever provided with the chance to do so. Then of course, there's the obvious damage being done to the ozone layer.

Now here's something that may surprise you, did you know that the air we breathe is twenty-one per cent oxygen, and if it was just two per cent lower than we wouldn't be able to breath. However, if it was just two per cent higher, then anything that happened to catch fire would burn uncontrollably.

Therefore, it goes to show just how fragile the balance between life and death actually is. So maybe some people need to rethink and change their perspective on life and the way they look at this beautiful world, and then maybe we just might see some changes for the better. Well you never know, maybe some big government chappie or chappesse I'm not that fussy about which one, decides that enough is enough, and keeps kicking up such a fuss until something is done.

Right then, back to global warming. Apparently, some top scientists are saying that the original calculations on global warming are wrong, because according to them the polar ice caps are not melting quickly enough.

Well personally, I'm not too upset by this revelation, in fact, very much the opposite, and quite pleased by this news. Providing of course this scientist's calculations are correct, now what's the betting some other suitably qualified scientist will come along and say that these calculations are also wrong?

(So we are none the wiser really) well as far as I can see there's a very simple answer to this dilemma and I did mention it earlier on, it's called sticking your head out the front door, opening your eyes and looking around. Because you really don't need fancy maths to see that something is drastically wrong here, I mean its just common sense really isn't it. I wonder if they could use these fancy maths to help us find a solution to global warming, well we can only hope can't we, unfortunately, I think we need to do quite a bit more than just hoping now.

Right then let's move on to the next subject, which is the over fishing of our oceans, because since the 1950's fishing catches have increased fivefold, from eighteen to one hundred million metric tons a year. And three quarters of fishing grounds are either exhausted, depleted, or are extremely close to it. Most of the large fish have been fished into extinction simply because we never gave them time to recover or time breed, and all the remaining fish are now also in very serious danger of being permanently wiped out.

Yet they still send out these giant ships with massive nets some of which are a couple of miles long. And each of these giant ships catch an average of fifty four thousand fish every hour, (along with anything else that gets caught up in the giant nets) which is a phenomenal amount. Now a great number of these fish and other creatures that end up in these massive nets are not wanted although all perfectly edible. Simply because it's not classed as a good fish to eat by whoever happens to be the world's number one chef that day.

Or the EU have said the fishermen are not allowed to catch them because they have a quota to work to, so all of these dead and surplus to requirements fish and other assorted creatures are thrown back into the ocean, fifty million tonnes of them to be precise, are thrown away each year.

Now as I mentioned earlier, the problem here is if we keep fishing the oceans at the same rate as we are today then in a mere forty years maximum from now (2012) there won't be any commercially viable fish left to catch.

The human population is increasing and the fish numbers are rapidly decreasing, now fish are the staple diet of one in five people yet we are still throwing millions of tonnes of them away what I don't understand is why? If you've killed them then surely you might as well eat them otherwise, it's just a waste. Now I can fully understand and even condone the need to control the amount of fish being caught however, we can all see that the fishing quota is just not doing what it was specifically designed by some top brain to do.

(Surely, thanks to our "superior intelligence" we should be capable of realising this) better still devise another and better way of catching the fish you want and avoiding the ones you don't want, because apparently these big trawlers use different size nets to catch certain fish. Plus they use state of the art radar systems to find the fish their looking for; nevertheless, as I said, people could consume the majority of these fish; for example, anchovies contain pretty much the same amount of protein as any other fish. However, because anchovies are not deemed "fashionable" enough to go on some top gourmets table they rarely get used.

Now I strongly believe that every living thing on this planet has a reason for being here, and are as I said, like the spokes in a bicycle wheel. Because these creatures have all evolved together over thousands or even millions of years to find its own little niche such as the best place to live which also provides in abundance the best food for them to eat. Therefore, if you interfere with one part of this food chain it will have a knock on effect to the rest of it normally for the worse, not the better. Here's a very good example of this happening for you to think about. In one part of the world possibly Mexico, where the local population of hammerhead sharks that once thrived there have practically been wiped out by over fishing, thanks mostly due to the tourist trade and to a certain extent the local fishermen.

Now because of this, there has been an absolute explosive increase in the number of the cow nosed rays that live in that area simply because its main predator the hammerhead shark, is no longer there to eat them and therefore keep their numbers under control.

Now this is not a one off incident by any means, because the same sort of thing has also happened in Monterey bay in America where hunters near enough wiped out the local population of sea otters by hunting them for their fur. And because of this, the population of sea urchins in that area exploded and thanks to the increase in its numbers the sea urchins have practically destroyed the giant kelp forests in that area, which was bad news for the local population of fish who depended on the giant kelp for their food and also for protection.

So no kelp forest meant no fish, so many of the local trawler men went out of business, however thankfully, some of the sea otters managed to survive, admittedly more through luck than judgement and they are now making a very strong comeback and have been classed as a protected species. So things are again starting to balance themselves out once more. And thankfully from this humanity have learned a valuable lesson.

Also in another part of the world where the local squid population has exploded, again because the sharks that normally eat them have practically disappeared.

Now although sharks have been given a really bad name mainly thanks to some crap films that were made about then in the 1980's we need to understand their purpose in the oceans of this world, because they play a very important part in helping the eco system stay in balance by keeping the population of our oceans in check.

(The cow nosed ray being a prime example) now as I said the sharks have been getting the blame for many things, but they are struggling for survival just the same as the many other creatures that are unfortunate enough to have a "valuable commodity" label placed on them. Because in the Indian Ocean the local shark population are being wiped out by the local fishermen who are killing over a thousand of them each year just for their fins, which they then sell to be used in Chinese restaurants for shark fin soup. However, the shark fin on its own doesn't taste of anything and has no natural flavour to it whatsoever, so the restaurants are adding some chicken broth to the soup to give it some flavour.

So the truth of the matter is these sharks are being killed for nothing. Therefore, the people who buy shark fin soup are really paying well over the top prices for a bowl of chicken soup with a bit of shark floating about in it.

Nevertheless, unfortunately for the sharks these restaurants are willing to pay a lot of money for them, because six shark fins are the equivalent to one year's wages for these fishermen, and of course, in order to feed their families the fishermen are going to make the most of it while they can.

However if they used their heads and placed a daily limit on how many sharks they could catch thereby giving the sharks a chance to recover and to breed then the fishermen could have a regular income instead of being greedy and killing the goose that lays the golden egg. Let's go back to the over fishing of our oceans for a moment. Because in an attempt to combat the over fishing problem, some bright spark came up with the idea of opening some fish farms, so we could breed our own fish for the table in a sustainable environment.

What a brilliant idea (in theory) but unfortunately not so good in practice, because the fish they decided to use to feed these farmed fish were caught out at sea. It's our old friend the anchovies, so we are back to throwing the "surplus to requirements" back into the sea, (dead of course) which I think completely defeats the idea of fish farming.

I would have thought it would have been common sense to breed the food before you started breeding the fish for the table furthermore, if you grind down sixty per cent anchovies you only get forty per cent fishmeal, so you automatically lose twenty per cent straight away. And, as I mentioned earlier we have already reached and passed the maximum number we could ever catch.

So in other words every time they catch these anchovies (or for that matter any other fish) the amount caught will get smaller and smaller with each and every catch made.

Therefore, in theory, it was a good idea, and I dare say if they had put a bit more effort, and thought into it, and bred the fish food first, then I dare say this idea would have worked a treat. Then we would have had all our table fish coming from a renewable source.

This of course would have been brilliant and would have given the oceans and their inhabitants a very much-needed rest, and a chance to recover and regain their natural balance once again.

They have also tried fish farming out at sea, because there are over forty blue fin tuna farms operating in the Mediterranean Sea, where between twenty to thirty thousand tonnes of these tuna are caught every year and are then kept in net pens until needed which was intended to take the strain off the blue fin tuna.

However, an average of twenty thousand tonnes of these tuna are undersize, so are therefore being caught illegally and because of this instead of helping the blue fin tuna they are now pushing them steadily towards extinction.

Now dolphins are believed to be one of the most intelligent creatures living in the oceans, and the bottlenose dolphin are the most widespread and best known in the world. They live in extended family groups known as pods, which are made up of aunts and other associated females. Now baby dolphins stay with their mother for the first two years of their life, and the milk produced by the mother is six times richer than cow's milk and this incredibly rich diet enables the young dolphin to double in size in just one month.

Now dolphins have excellent eyesight but they also have another very clever way of "seeing" because they are capable of beaming sound waves from their

The Entelligent Idiot

foreheads. They then use the returning echoes to create a picture in sound, this sonar penetrates like an x-ray and they use it to find whatever food may be hiding in the sand on the ocean floor, they can even tell what type of creature's hiding beneath the sand. They can also use sonar to stun its prey, and by concentrating the intensity of the clicks, they can penetrate deeper into the sand.

Now every dolphin has its own unique signature whistle, which it uses as its name, now pod members come and go as they please, yet no matter how long the members have been away they always seem to recognize each other by sight, as well as by their signature whistle.

The male dolphins live in bachelor pods away from the females and just like the female pods male members come and go pretty much as they please, but it seems the friendship they have with each other is there for life.

Now we all know how dolphins love to jump, and they can reach a height of six metres (twenty feet) and they just can't resist the temptation to show off as they somersault, and spin just for the sheer fun of it.

Then you have the more energetic spinner dolphins that are more than capable of covering two hundred and fifty miles in a single day. And the reason they are called spinner dolphins is because they just love to spin as fast as they possibly can as they leap from the water, and no other dolphin can achieve these incredible corkscrews, it's also believed that the rapid spinning could also help to dislodge aquatic parasites.

These dolphins normally travel in small pods, however occasionally they come together to form super pods that can contain several hundred of them and can be over a mile long. Which may sound a lot however, on some occasions they can form what's commonly known as a mega pod and this pod can contain as many as three thousand dolphins or more.

Now these clever dolphins can be quite cunning in the ways of catching its prey, one of which is sending dolphins ahead of the shoal of fish they are hunting, then they surround the shoal with a wall of muddy water by whipping the shallow ocean floor with their tails.

Then they just wait for the fish to jump out of the water to escape the trap and the dolphins just catch them in mid-air. Now apparently dolphins can hear a shoal of fish from as far as ten miles away, then once they catch up with them they scan each fish in the shoal, as they look for the old or the weak that are moving slower and are therefore easier to catch.

They also like to use the coral reefs as a makeshift health spa in order to remove any old bits of skin. And they have a tendency to use the same rocks or coral on every visit, which is quite frequent because amazingly dolphins replace the outer layer of its skin every three hours. Which when you think about it is a vital requirement for an animal where streamlining is everything, so rubbing themselves against the rocks helps to speed up the process and just like us, they appear to enjoy nothing more than having a really good scratch.

Now being an intelligent and very curious creature they quite often become bored, and are always on the lookout for something new to do or to explore. Which surprisingly enough also includes surfing, and just like the professional human surfers they know exactly the right time to hit a wave for its maximum power, and unlike any other animal (apart from ourselves) they do it just for the fun of it. They also like us are one of the few animals that have sex for pleasure and not just for reproduction.

And as I mentioned earlier juvenile groups of dolphins have been seen chewing on puffer fish and passing it around to its companions simply to get high on the toxins produced by the puffer fish in order to scare their predators away. Also due to their constant curiosity and searching for something to do, just helps the intelligence of these wonderful creatures to grow.

Now the next topic I think will both shock and disgust you. Because the Japanese kill on average twenty three thousand dolphins and porpoises each and every year, now admittedly the majority of the Japanese people know absolutely nothing about this and are completely oblivious to this annual slaughter, thanks to a complete and total media ban.

Although there have been numerous attempts made to secretly film this so called "culling" as far as I can tell only one documentary has ever been successfully made about it, and you can literally watch the water turn red with the blood of these beautiful creatures.

Now there aren't that many people in the world that are willing to eat porpoise or dolphin meat. However, it's not because of the old television series about a dolphin that lived in Australia, or the fact they look cute and are extremely friendly towards humans actively seeking and enjoying our company, plus they also have that "knowing" look in their eyes.

However, the reason people won't eat dolphin meat is because of its high mercury content, so what I would like to know is what exactly happens to this mountain of meat, and where does it go? Because that's an awful lot of dead bodies to dispose of, well strangely enough nobody appears to know the answer to this question.

This unnecessary slaughter happens at the same time and same place every year in a small village named Taiji. Where people chase the porpoise and dolphins inland with the use of speedboats, they then trap these defenceless creatures in a secluded cove and then the slaughter begins supposedly humanely with knives and harpoons, which doesn't sound very humane to me somehow.

However, these people have also been seen using clubs, and even hammers to bludgeon these poor creatures to a slow and painful death I've heard a recording of their screams it sounds like a scalded baby it really is disgusting. So what reason could they possibly have to justify this mass slaughter?

Well believe it or not as far as these people are concerned they're not doing anything wrong and are just culling them as a form of pest control, because apparently these porpoises and dolphins are eating too many fish! Which doesn't appear to me to be anywhere near a legitimate or valid reason somehow, because we don't rely solely on fish as our main or staple food source, whereas the dolphins and porpoise do.

Furthermore, we can pop down to the shop and purchase food from anywhere in the world, whereas the dolphins (obviously) have to catch theirs, plus the fact we throw away fifty million tonnes of fish each year.

So personally, I class the Japanese reason as just another feeble excuse in an attempt to justify something they know only to well to be wrong, and the same thing applies to their whaling for "scientific research" which thankfully has now apparently been banned.

Furthermore, we already know who's really responsible for the fish shortage but as usual, we prefer to blame some innocent creature rather than face the truth and accept the responsibility ourselves.

Now this carnage starts every September, and continues right up until the end of March, so that's a solid six months of killing these lovely creatures just for the sake of it. There is absolutely no reason for these people to take part in this disgusting ritual, it has to be stopped and completely abolished immediately, humanity

The Entelligent Idiot

possesses both the intelligence and the laws to prevent this needless slaughter from ever happening again. And in New Zealand there's an Organization called the WDC, which stands for the Whale and Dolphin Conservation, are doing their utmost to stop net fishing in known whale and dolphin areas because they keep getting trapped in the nets and are therefore drowning. Now the New Zealand dolphins were already struggling and now their numbers have reached critical levels now the New Zealand dolphin is the worlds smallest dolphin, and they are also known as Hectors dolphins and sadly there are only four surviving populations left, and they live in the shallow coastal waters around New Zealand. However these little dolphins are heading for extinction because over one hundred of them are drowned in the fishing nets each year. Which means they are dying quicker than they can breed so in just a few short years from now these dolphins could be gone forever which I think would be a terrible shame. Yet despite all the efforts of the WDC the New Zealand government are still refusing to ban this form of fishing in the designated areas so please log on to their website and sign their petition, and I sincerely wish the WDC nothing but success.

However, it seems to me that man just can't be bothered to do anything about it, and just turns a blind eye to this disgusting slaughter, as it would be too much effort, along with our why do today what you can do tomorrow sort of attitude that's got us in this predicament in the first place. However, I bet it would be a very different story if it involved oil, gas or minerals, and this is what wound me up enough to write this book in the first place.

Because if enough people agree with what I've written here, and I believe there's an awful lot of people that will, if they all started asking questions and lobbied their respective members of parliament and refuse to believe any more of their political bullshit.

Then hopefully people will finally realize that they can practically force the government of this world to create and implement the new laws and changes needed. Simply by keeping the pressure on them, (nagging) well it works for my wife.

Seriously though it really is just a matter of keeping the pressure on them, and refusing to take no for an answer because no government in the world wants bad or negative publicity. Furthermore, they really do need to stop making these pathetic little reassuring noises such as well we really are trying our utmost; the only thing being tried is people's patience. And they also insult people's intelligence, by believing that we really are stupid and gullible enough to believe these sad little stories they concoct in their effort to convince us otherwise.

If only they put as much effort into sorting out our problems, as they do into their pathetic little excuses I wouldn't have had to write this book. And everyone would be living happily ever after in a world where the sun always shine's, and there's no wars or famine, no corruption, where nothing bad ever happens. Unfortunately for us, we don't live in an ideal and perfect fairy-tale world. Although I dare say, there are some surprisingly large amounts of people who truly believe they do, and they believe they can do whatever they want because it doesn't really matter, and whatever they do won't adversely affect anything, and the world will miraculously heal itself overnight and will last forever.

Now of course those of us that have to live in the real world know this will never happen (unfortunately) although I dare say if the strain was taken off this planet it would eventually start to heal itself to a certain extent, with of course some help from us.

Which wouldn't be a bad idea really, because the only thing mankind has ever done from day one is take from this planet, and I think it's time to start giving something back as a way of saying thankyou to this unique world for everything she's given us. And it really is long overdue, so why don't we do it and find out for ourselves. Although I must admit, I have thoroughly enjoyed writing this book, (and getting it off my chest) in addition, I have learned so much about the state of our poor and through no fault of her own bedraggled and tattered planet, some of which is quite scary. Now I don't pretend to have, or know all or any of the answers to these questions, quite simply because I don't. However, what I am hoping is this little book may put a few ideas' forward that could be used or adapted by someone to help in solving our problem, or maybe even give the top brains something to consider or possibly help point them in the right direction.

Alternatively, even get them to look at our problems from a completely different angle, and possibly find a simpler solution, for a start they could demand that the carbon emissions are reduced to the recommended levels worldwide.

Because let's be honest, they do go around in circles chasing their own tails quite a lot don't they. Along with the other bad habit of "going of half cocked" a very good example of this was the fish farm scheme.

In theory which is what these top brains are good at, it is a really good idea (on paper) however, in practice, which you must admit they're not always too good at, it turns out to be completely unworkable, simply because not enough thought went into it during the planning process.

Just because the problem appears at first glance to be very complex, and of course a lot of the time they are. However, that doesn't automatically mean the solution to the problem also needs to be complex.

And sometimes you need to look at things with a childlike vision and a more simplistic eye, because surprisingly enough more often than not it appears to be the best approach, unfortunately, we also have a habit of "under thinking" things, for example if you're going to breed something for food then it will also need to be fed. So common sense should tell you you'll need to organize a renewable food source for whatever it is you intend to breed before you start breeding it, any farmer would have told them this.

In addition, the same principal applies to the rainforest's problem's, the government will send in some top brains in an attempt to solve them and I dare say at considerable expense to us the humble taxpayer for this expert's valuable time and experience. Furthermore, it would probably take them months to find out something that the locals would have told them on their very first day of arrival if they'd only asked.

Or they could put organizations such as Greenpeace, Friends of the earth and the WWF in complete charge of all funds, let them also be responsible for saying who does what, where, and when, as I dare say we all know if you need to find something out then go straight to the "grass roots" of the community. Because these people already know what and where the problems are in addition, and more importantly, more often than not they will also know the people responsible for creating these problems in the first place.

Furthermore, I wouldn't be at all surprised if many of the local people would offer to help in any way they could, for example by recommending people for recruitment for various jobs such as patrolling known trouble areas, administration, making people aware of what's going on, etc.

Now here's a bit of good news for a change, you may remember that earlier on I mentioned that SKY TV had teamed up with the WWF to raise money to buy up certain areas of the rainforest. Well I have since discovered that a well-known chocolate manufacturer has followed their example and have started a similar scheme, which is also intended to help the rainforest.

In addition, another well-known "household name" company that manufactures toilet tissue who are planting three trees to replace each one they use have also become involved. And a very big thankyou goes to them all for their time, concern, commitment, and willingness to help. I just hope all the other companies will follow their lead, even if it's just out of feeling obligated to do so or even as a part of their advertising campaign, because it would obviously do them more good than harm.

The company's public relations officer certainly should have already known this, because a surprisingly large number of people would take this into consideration when buying similar products.

Yes, I know that to some people this may sound a bit on the callous side because it sounds like I'm condoning using the plight of the Rainforest to sell products however, if it helps to raise funding through donations from these companies, along with raising people's awareness of what's going on then surely that must be a good thing. Because as I said earlier if enough people get involved then hopefully the governments of this world will also feel obligated, to show some support and involvement.

Because now these companies have started the ball rolling and many more people are now having their eyes opened to what is really going on in the world around them, and they are also discovering that they can help to make a big difference.

Either by buying these companies products, making donations, signing online petitions, and even boycotting other companies products because they don't make any donations and are also more than likely to be a major contributor to most of the pollution.

Or you could possibly decide to do all of them because honestly it really would make a big difference. Then I believe these schemes would quickly gather momentum and hopefully our problems would be solved or at least help pave the way towards a solution.

Therefore, we can only hope the governments of this world will also feel guilty enough to get involved.

Now as strange as it may sound I really do have a good feeling about this, (especially if we keep nagging at them) and we can now see a light at the end of this long tunnel let's just hope it's someone with the solution to our problem, and the sooner they show up the better. And not some idiot's who want to cause trouble.

Now apparently some of our top brains think they may have solved our shortage of housing problem in one foul swoop because some bright spark has come up with the novel idea of building some huge skyscrapers, well nothing new there then I hear you say.

However, these skyscrapers are not just for people to live in, oh no, because they intend to build an entire city in these buildings. Therefore, you would never have to leave these wonderful structures, because (according to them) everything you could ever need in your entire lifetime will have been incorporated into these "tower block cities."

Okay that's fine. However, could someone please enlighten me as to the whereabouts in this "ground breaking advancement in modern technology" do they intend to place the graveyard, in the basement maybe? (That's what the leaf cutter ants and termites use in their colonies, which is basically, what these tower block cities would be, human colonies) so that's another "dumb animal" that has taught us something.

Oh and one more thing, these buildings would have to be colossal in size so how do you get from one end to the other? Unless of course you can drive your car in there but even if you could where would you park it? And if you are allowed to drive in these buildings (which I very much doubt) because you would then just be adding to your problems because you would obviously need to get rid of the exhaust fumes, unless of course the residents will only be allowed to drive either electric or hydrogen cell cars?

But in all probability, they would have to use the electric cars simply because they don't give out any emissions, although saying that, the hydrogen cell cars emissions are only water vapour so maybe they could also use that to help supply the drinking water. Because Scientists are now predicting the world will suffer from water shortages in the not to distant future.

Now the how will you get about question may sound like a minor detail to many people unless of course you are unfortunately disabled and can't walk.

They are also talking about building vast subterranean cities, which of course mean people would be living underground; now both of these ideas strike me as being a bit on the scary, impractical, and somewhat desperate side, has enough thought gone into the planning of these structures? I doubt it, but hopefully yes it has.

(Remember the fish farm fiasco) also if you intend to live underground how are you going to get your supply of lighting, heating, water and waste disposal down there?

More importantly, what are they going to use to generate this energy, which would be quite a substantial amount? It would also be a pointless exercise if they intended to use fossil fuels because we all know these resources are rapidly running out.

Maybe they could use the vast amounts of waste they'd produce each day. Because I certainly would not want a nuclear reactor as my next-door neighbour some how would you? I don't care how safe they say they are.

(Plus they're not the ones living next door to the thing) I really can't see people fighting for the privilege of being one of the first people to live down there.

However, having said that, you never know, because there are a surprisingly large number of people who are gullible enough to believe every word the government say in an attempt to convince everyone that this idea is the best thing since sliced bread, and is the answer to all our housing problems.

But then if that's right then it would be interesting to see just how many members of parliament will have a subterranean second home that they'll actually use, and not just as a publicity stunt. Now even if they do build this subterranean city and manage to get it right on the first attempt, I think if I had to choose between one or the other, I believe I would rather live in one of the new super deluxe "tower block cities" which they claim will be "built with you in mind." However, all these big plans still sound a bit on the desperate side to me.

And very much like a drowning man clutching at straws So really, all of these big put the world to right schemes could well be, and most probably will be a complete and utter waste of time and taxpayers money.

Because obviously, the people who devise these schemes don't do so because their either bored, or out of the kindness of their hearts, they do it because they get paid very large amounts of money, for their "inspirational and ground breaking designs", and I dread to think exactly how much was paid for this little lot.

Okay now I recently found out a bit more on these underground cities and such like, the people of Amsterdam are planning to build some colossal underground car parks, which I believe to be a good idea.

Also apparently, the Russians intend to build a giant underground shopping centre in Moscow and fair play to them. And now for the cherry on the cake, which is in America, because they are planning to build a huge underground city directly below the original city of Chicago? (Which seems a bit strange) it would be approximately one thousand and three hundred feet directly below the existing city.

Furthermore, they would have to remove two hundred and thirty million square yards of soil and stone to create this city, now that's an awful lot of rubbish to dispose of once it's been excavated. Then of course, you'll need to get a constant supply of fresh air down there, which to be honest wouldn't be a major problem, and should be fairly easy to do, (being an ex-coalminer I understand ventilation requirements.) Now as far as I can tell there are two fundamental problems here.

The main one being, how they intend to stop the old city that's directly above, from sinking and crushing the new one below? This is what made me somewhat sceptical of the plan to build it directly underneath the old city in the first place. The other problem is getting natural sunlight down there and recreating the natural movement of the sun and shadows.

This may not appear to be of much importance to you and me. Nevertheless, apparently it is a very crucial element for getting our "body clocks" to function normally.

Furthermore, I have been reliably informed that the temperature will stay constant at around fifty-five degrees centigrade (one hundred and thirty one degrees Fahrenheit) In addition, for every one hundred feet further down you go the temperature will increase by one degree, so no need to worry about heating the place, in fact very much the reverse.

Now this unwanted heat could also provide the answer to the "what will they use to produce the power" question that I mentioned earlier, because, if they could find a way of channelling this heat (which shouldn't be to difficult) then in theory, they could use it to rotate the blades on something similar to a wind turbine. The turbine could also be used as a pump to run the waste disposal unit to take the waste back to the surface to be disposed of sensibly. Or the more sensible thing to do which we should do with all of our waste, is it could be recycled to produce methane gas that could then be used by the general public.

Thereby killing two birds with one stone, or for those of you that aren't familiar with that term it means solving two problems at the same time, so there would be no need for fracking then?

(So that would be three birds then) it has to be worth a try surely. Furthermore, it could also be used to bring fresh air into the city, because as I dare say you already know as hot air rises up one shaft it would also pull fresh air down another shaft. (That's why a lot of coalmines had two shafts) now if they can do that and I don't see any reason why they can't, then I have to admit that it could well be a feasible idea. (And I never thought I would say that) especially if the intention is too eventually, have every one of us living underground, which really would not, surprise me in the slightest.

Although I must admit, I am still somewhat sceptical about the whole idea, because as I mentioned these top brains are really good at the theory bit of it, but unfortunately, they are not so good at the practical side of things, now admittedly they don't always get it wrong, just wrong quite a bit of the time.

Nevertheless, even if they were right it's still not going to solve anything is it? Because there is still one not so small problem that appears to have been forgotten, or conveniently left out of this equation, and that is of course global warming.

With the polar ice caps melting and the resulting rise in sea levels because water expands when it's heated and just in the twentieth century alone levels have increased by twenty centimetres. In addition, the ever increasing and very real threat of entire cities being permanently lost to the sea in the next twenty to thirty years. So unfortunately, and with that thought in mind I really don't think I would be too keen on living in an underground city, possibly with a nuclear reactor as my next-door neighbour. So that appears to have put a bit of a damper on the whole idea really, pardon the pun.

Oh talking of increasing sea levels, some top brain came up with the idea of building some "floating cities" the intention of building these floating cities is to counteract the rising sea levels around the world therefore, these cities would obviously be permanently out at sea. Now apparently these cities would be just the same as any land-based city complete with roads, cars, Lorries, trains and so on, and each one would be capable of linking together like some kind of giant jigsaw. Each individual piece so it seems would be fitted with its own engines and rudder so they have a choice of linking with another city or they could just sail off under their own power. However, I believe the general idea is to link them all together to improve its strength and stability.

These floating cities would stay out at sea the majority of the time, and apparently, this is where they would also catch the bulk of their food, so they wouldn't have to come in to land very often.

However, catching their food may not be as easy as they seem to think thanks to the ever-dwindling number of fish left in the oceans of this world.

Furthermore, there's one other thing I would be very concerned about if I happened to be living on one of these floating cities. Which is of course the ever-increasing extreme weather conditions we are experiencing, because I really wouldn't want to be on one of them when it could be hit by a massive tsunami type wave.

Or alternatively, a one hundred mile an hour Cyclone, because there is no way on this earth these floating cities could outrun either of them, which is a very daunting thought to say the least.

However, they did have a scaled down model built to show just how these things would work so they were seriously considering this scheme but hopefully the plans showing how to build these floating cities will remain in a locked draw (or the recycling bin) where they belong. But I have a strange feeling they will surface again one-day pardon the pun.

Oh, here's one more thing to think about. What do you personally believe should be first on our list of top priorities? Creating vast underground or floating cities that no one would ever live in, or finding a solution to global warming and its associated problems. Now if you still cant work out the answer to that one, then can I just say this, could the last person alive please turn the lights of the world off before you die thankyou?

The Entellingent Idiot

Now I recently discovered that the sun should last for at least another five billion years before it goes "belly up" and dies, which is a long time by anyone's standards. Although unfortunately, I really cant see our species lasting that long somehow, unless there are some serious changes made, and soon. I also recently discovered that in one hour, the sun gives the earth the same amount of energy as consumed by humanity in one year, and if it was harnessed properly we would quite literally have an endless and completely limitless source of free energy, which would also be pollutant free. But of course the big coal, oil, and gas companies don't want that to happen because they would then lose everything because we would no longer have a need for their products.

Now many people have attempted to solve the riddle of finding the best way of producing free renewable energy with various degrees of success over the years; now in 2007 a company built the largest tide turbine in the world and they installed it in a loch in Ireland.

I suppose the best way to describe this tide turbine is to call it an upside down windmill, although it doesn't look anything like one, but the principal is basically the same. (No offence meant or intended to the inventor and designer of this turbine by that statement mind) now as I said they have placed the turbine in a loch in Ireland, the turbine is situated in the narrowest part of the loch in order to maximize the water flow, the water then turns the turbines blades, and generates electricity.

Now this turbine, being the first of its kind is obviously a prototype. However, it's capable of producing between seven hundred and fifty, and one thousand five hundred kilowatts. That's enough electricity to power one thousand homes, which is excellent, in addition, they intend to start producing these water turbines on a large scale in the not too distant future and these water turbines could soon be producing as much as ten megawatts.

However, if they can get the right financial backing and regulatory framework they could be producing up to five hundred megawatts by the year 2015, which I personally think is absolutely brilliant. It would also be an excellent opportunity for the government to step in and make it look as if they care by making certain the company receives all the financial and regulatory help they need

And to assure them of their willingness to help them succeed in getting these turbines into production as soon as possible now this company are by no means on its own in this search for alternative energy supplies.

Because there is another company which is based in Scotland that have come up with another way of harnessing the tidal energy of the sea which they've named the Anaconda, simply because it looks like a really big snake.

And this "big snake" consists mainly of a mix of fabric and rubber, it sits in the sea and the movement of the waves turns a turbine that's built into the snakes tail thereby generating the electricity. A two hundred metre one would produce enough to power one thousand homes and apparently, if used properly all of these different types of water turbines could produce most, if not all of this country's energy needs.

So why haven't our government officials been busy beating a path to their doors, and offering to help them in any way they can to get these turbines into production as quickly as the red tape would allow? Unfortunately, the answer to that question sadly eludes me, however, I dare say it'll be profit related somewhere along the line.

Now I know I keep saying this, but I really cannot understand the mentality of these people in government.

The Entelligent Idiot

Could it be they're just sat there, waiting for the inventors of these remarkable machines, which they have worked so hard to devise, design and build, to walk through their office door with one of their water turbines for them to inspect. So that the government official doesn't have to get out of the nice comfortable chair they're sat in, just to waste their time looking at something as trivial as the possible solution to our problem.

This also explains how I came to think of the title for this book The Intelligent Idiot, because undoubtedly it is what we are.

Now staying with the theory of new ways to create and supply renewable energy, someone in Amsterdam has come up with a novel idea of using kites to produce electricity. Now obviously these are not the same sort of kites you would fly on the beach with your children.

The kites they intend to use would be huge, and they would be made out of Kevlar, Which is a very strong material it's used in the manufacturing of bullet-proof vests for the armed forces and the metropolitan police. Now these kites would need to be very robust indeed, because they intend to send the kites ten kilometres (just over six miles) up into the upper atmosphere where you have winds travelling at speeds of three hundred and twenty one kilometres (two hundred miles) an hour and more.

Now the theory is, as the wind pulls the kite the cable attached to it would rotate a large drum therefore generating the electricity. Which sounds okay although I would be rather concerned about an aeroplane flying into the cables along with the possibility of strikes by lightening, although I dare say they would intend to create a no flying zone in that area. And maybe they could find a way of channelling the lightning strikes so they could use the electricity that's produced? This would make sense; I'm surprised no one has found a way to do it.

And now back to England, well to Oxford to be a bit more precise, because there they are learning how to create, control, and harness nuclear fusion, which is also what powers the sun.

Now apparently nuclear fusion is a lot safer to use than nuclear reaction, so if they can master this process then great, although I must admit it all sounds a bit complex to a mere mortal such as myself. Nevertheless, I will do my best to explain it, right then in a nutshell, nuclear reaction splits atoms, whereas nuclear fusion joins atoms together and thereby creating energy.

Unfortunately, the complex bit is they have to heat the atoms up until they become the same temperature as the sun, and they then use magnets to control it. So in reality their creating a mini sun I suppose. Now the temperature on the surface of the sun (photosphere) is five thousand five hundred degrees Celsius. However, in the centre (core) it's an incredible fifteen million degrees Celsius. Nevertheless, they have managed to create this mini sun however unfortunately; they haven't been able to sustain it for any longer than thirty seconds at the moment, although I have no doubt they will soon find a solution to this problem.

Right then we're now off to Albuquerque in America because two people that live there have discovered a way of producing petrol out of fresh air and water.

And as unbelievable, as that may sound these people have actually accomplished it. They used carbon dioxide and water, then they heat them up to a temperature of two thousand four hundred degrees centigrade, which they do with the use of the sun and some mirrors, which is a brilliant idea.

However, the maximum they can produce at this moment is only two or three gallons each day (I wonder what the exhaust emissions would be like?)

Now here's a thought what if they used the heat they produce to make this petrol for another purpose for example using the heat they generate to turn a rotor similar to a wind turbine. Alternatively, steam or something along those lines, and because the heat they produce is free I would have thought it could also be used for other things. And I can't see any reason why they couldn't build these machines in various locations throughout the world because we have vast areas of empty desert where they could place these machines, because as I said the sun gives the earth in one hour the same amount of energy as humanity consume in one year.

We could also use these deserts for solar panels, I mean potentially the uses they could find for this free resource are endless, and you can place the machines practically anywhere there's strong sunlight. Now if you think about it a nuclear reactor generates electricity from the heat that's produced.

Therefore, couldn't they use this new and free heat source to do the same job? However, without the obvious dangers that come with nuclear reactors, surely it has to be worth looking into because a large number of inventions are discovered by accident.

Now if you sit down and think about man's intelligence just remember one thing, mankind has gone from the earliest of car's the model T ford to the space shuttle in a mere seventy-five years which in reality is just a blink of an eye compared to how long we have actually been living on this planet.

I just wonder if humanity would ever put the same amount of energy and effort into restoring this beautiful planet to its former glory, and possibly even improve it. Personally speaking I believe it is possible and obviously well worth doing.

Nevertheless, for some reason that sadly escapes me humanity doesn't appear even vaguely interested, or at best they will make a last minute attempt to put things right. Unfortunately, if it is left until the last minute then I fear the world will be changed forever and obviously not for the better, which worries me greatly.

So let's hope humanity decides to put things right sooner rather than later, furthermore I bet it wouldn't take seventy-five years to do so hopefully.

Now I mentioned earlier on about the sky/wwf efforts to get people to donate money to save the rainforest. And how they would match each donation made. Well they have now started similar schemes such as adopt a snow leopard, tiger, or polar bear etc. this is a brilliant idea. Now apparently some people have complained that not all of this donated money is being used to help the animal it was originally intended for.

And it's being used to help some really ugly and nasty insects and similar creatures that no one would be willing to sponsor nevertheless, these insects are an integral and very important part of the micro world and therefore the eco system, so they are still using this money for a very good purpose.

Now the next time you go to stamp on a spider or swat a fly here's a little something to remember before you do it which is, if all of mankind disappeared of the face of the earth tomorrow we wouldn't even be missed, and all life here would survive and even flourish.

Nevertheless, if every insect on this planet disappeared tomorrow then every single known life form on this planet would die. If the common and garden bumblebee's that pollinate seventy five per cent of all the plants that exist on this planet and are really struggling to survive at the moment due to the over use of pesticides, if they disappeared then humanity would be struggling to survive within as little as four months. Now bumblebees pollinate a very wide range of commercial crops such as tomatoes, peas, apples, strawberries etc, and insects are estimated to contribute over four hundred million pounds each year to the United Kingdoms economy, and just over fourteen billion euros a year to the EU economy so we really do need to protect them.

Friends of the Earth are trying to raise money, which they will then use to create bee friendly environments in the countryside and in the cities, towns, and villages all across the country, where they will plant wild flowers that attract bees in order to give them a safe haven. If you go on their website Friends of the Earth.com they will send you a free packet of seeds to encourage the bees into your garden, they'll ask if you can make a donation and if you can then they would be very grateful because like many other charitably run organizations they need all the help they can get. I have already received and planted my seeds. And I have also followed their advice and made a bumble bee drinking tray which is basically using something similar to a shallow baking tray or dish and filling it with marbles and topping it up with water until it's just below the top of the marbles so the bees have something to land on.

Because when the bees try to drink from a bird bath unfortunately quite a few of them drown.

Did you know that it would take twelve honeybees their entire lifetime to make just one teaspoonful of honey?

Furthermore, the same can be said for the phytoplankton that I mentioned earlier, so I believe humanity really needs to sit down and seriously rethink its "surplus to requirements" strategy. Because believe it or not, the only creature that really is "surplus to requirements" on this planet is in fact us, which of course many people will vigorously, deny, because many people still believe Global warming is just some sort of a practical joke to frighten people which is a very sobering thought.

And therefore the most important things on the planet are what we like to call the so-called "lower" life forms such as the algae, plankton, and the insects.

So humanity through an over inflated ego and vanity has once more proven without a doubt that we really aren't the sharpest knife in the draw. Because every other life form on this planet appears to respect Mother Nature, and they are quite happy to live by her rules. Whereas mankind's "big businesses" are hell bent on sucking every last bit of oil, coal, and gas out of this world and have no intention of stopping until they have destroyed everything, including all of humanity, and the very planet itself. So let's put it into prospective.

All the other animals that share this planet with us are "dumb" enough to respect what they've got, and we are "intelligent" enough to destroy it, which as I said earlier doesn't really strike me as the most intelligent thing to do somehow, surely no one could disagree with that statement? Yet you can practically guarantee some will, even though the majority of humanity suffers needlessly, just for the benefit of such a few.

Now earlier I mentioned how we send our recycled rubbish to Gambia, well I have since discovered what happens to this rubbish once it reaches its final destination. They take it to a rubbish tip that stretches for several miles then its dumped and just left wherever it lands, because there's not much in the way of organization on this rubbish tip they don't even attempt to bury it.

The Entelligent Idiot

Now there are people and even entire families, (some of which were born there) permanently living on this rubbish tip, they also sleep out in the open in all weathers, except for the few that have managed to make some sort of makeshift shelter out of the huge piles of rubbish that surrounds them.

Most of them (which also includes small children) don't have any shoes. And they have to walk barefoot through all of this rubbish, which includes broken glass, sharp bits of rusty metal, and god only knows what else that's sticking up through the ground as they rummage through this rubbish, in their search for any scrap metal such as copper wire and aluminium. Along with any clothes, shoes, bedding, or anything and everything else they may be able to sell as they attempt to make some kind of meagre living from all of this rubbish.

Unfortunately when they burn the copper wire in an attempt to remove the plastic outer casing they are breathing in toxic fumes. There is one unfortunate little boy who is just ten years old yet his voice is really deep which is caused by breathing in these toxic fumes. Plus he suffers with severe chest problems also caused by the fumes he breathes in on a daily basis, and just to complicate the situation even further his parents can't afford to get him any medical treatment.

So unfortunately, this little boy's future through no fault of his own doesn't look to promising to say the least.

Now all of this rubbish is there thanks to our constant need to have the latest model out, and new upgrades most of the computer's still have the local government stamps on them including county council, and even stuff from the constabulary. There's also a small mountain of stuff from our hospitals and clinics, so much for sensible recycling, and this is allowed to happen all thanks to a very convenient loophole in the law, that states if its "broken" which it obviously is or you wouldn't be throwing it away, it can go into a landfill site.

Therefore, the next time you get a snotty letter from your local council for not recycling your rubbish properly, I suggest you tell them ever so politely to go and recycle it.

Now for some good news on the conservation problem, as I mentioned earlier about the Orang Utan and young elephant sanctuaries well apparently they are now well known and have become a very popular tourist attraction. And the people who visit them pay a small admission fee to see the animals, and if they're interested they can get involved with feeding them and so forth.

Which I think is an excellent idea, because not only are the tourists helping fund a very important organization. They also get to learn why these unfortunate animals are there in the first place, which can't be a bad thing.

Now hopefully these tourists will go away with some long lasting and happy memories of their visit and maybe with a very different outlook on the world and the creatures that live here, because I believe if people became more aware of what is really happening to this world "behind their backs" then things would soon begin to change. Because these people would kick up enough fuss to get the governments and these giant companies to change the way they run their businesses, and possibly force them into making some fundamental and much needed changes, because lets be honest our world governments don't really tell us a lot do they.

I mean it's a no brainer really isn't it? Surely, these businesses must be able to see this or are they just turning a blind eye for their new God whose name just happens to be profit. In addition, remember this, as I said the governments of this world are there to serve us, whereas they appear to be under the illusion we are here to serve them (and as far back as anyone can remember we have been.) Now we need to explain to these people in no uncertain terms that this is no longer the case, and the quicker the error of their ways gets pointed out to them the better it will be for each and everyone of us.

Now I am not naïve enough to think this little book will change the world, however I hope it will help people change the way they look at this world, and hopefully get them thinking. And just as importantly, asking the question why haven't we done anything to put these things right and why weren't we told about it many years ago when it was originally discovered what was happening. Because if people keep on about it for long enough (nagging) then the Governments of this world will eventually be forced to do something about it, oh and did you spot the deliberate spelling mistake in the title on the front cover? No? This just goes to prove that not everything is as it first appears, and sometimes we need to look at things a little bit more closely.

Unfortunately, if we don't keep reminding them of this (nagging) then sadly nothing will ever change, and we will only have ourselves to blame.

So the corruption, manipulation, and lies would continue completely unchecked. So please don't just sit there thinking yes he's quite right in what he's saying, but I won't get involved because I expect someone else will do it, and they won't really want or need me, and I'm only one person so what possible difference could I make? Well actually, you could make a very big difference indeed, because if you only know one more person that thinks the same way about this world as you then you have the foundations for an organization that could make all the difference.

Alternatively, of course you could join, donate, or even volunteer your services to help one of the already established organizations, how do you imagine Greenpeace, Friends of the earth, or the wwf got started. So please do not underestimate the difference that you and people like you could make, humanity has long had the ability to communicate with each other, so let's put this ability along with our intelligence to good use because we all need to get together to stop this senseless onslaught of destruction dead in its tracks.

We also need to show the politicians and the world governments that they will no longer lead us blindly and it is our common law right to be able to have our say on all the important matters that will undoubtedly have a profound effect on each and every one of us.

Go to tpuc.com or google freeman of the land, it really is worth a look at. So please keep this in mind once you have finished reading this book. Furthermore, if you have read this book from cover to cover, then I would hazard a guess that you agree with some or hopefully all that I've written here, and maybe you feel as strongly about what's happening to our home as I do.

Now I will apologize in advance for saying this again but if we don't (peacefully) keep the pressure on the politicians and the big businesses then nothing will ever change, And as I said we will only have ourselves to blame. So please don't think oh, I'll leave it to someone else who knows what they're doing. Get involved, and enjoy the feeling of knowing you've accomplished something. So make yourself a cup of tea or coffee, then sit yourself down and have a long serious think and talk with your family and friends about what kind of world you would like your children and their children to grow up in. Humanity needs to realize that it has taken this planet billions of years to achieve the perfect balance that exists between all things that live here.

Yet humanity has practically destroyed this balance in a very short space of time.

Furthermore, unless there are some fundamental changes made very soon, then in a mere forty years from now 2012 (that's the maximum estimate) the majority of the polar ice caps will have melted away, so many of our cities and towns will be lost forever to the sea thanks to the rising sea levels.

The polar bears and other life forms that depend on these ice caps will more than probably be extinct, (except for those in the zoos) and by the year 2050, one quarter of all the animals living on this planet will be under serious threat of extinction. And at the moment one mammal in four, one bird in eight, and one amphibian in three are under a very real threat of extinction. And species are now dying out one thousand times faster than the natural rate. And as I said three quarters of the fishing grounds are now empty, so the majority of the fish that live in the oceans of this world will soon be extinct. Here's something else to think about, if you are now middle aged then during your lifetime, (from the day you were born up until the present day) a staggering fifty per cent of all known species have become extinct.

So the other thing I struggle to understand is, why the world governments spend billions of dollars every year on monitoring the Asteroid belt with giant telescopes and such like, as they constantly search the heavens for rogue asteroids that could possibly be on a head on collision course with the earth. And there's a minor planet monitoring centre in Boston Massachusetts whose sole job is to keep an eye on the seven thousand "near earth" Asteroids that orbit this planet. However, the main ones they appear to be looking for are anything over one kilometre in diameter.

Because a collision with one that size would be catastrophic for the planet because the shock waves alone would kill every living thing within a one hundred mile radius and there are over nine hundred of these asteroids in dangerous near earth orbits.

And one meteor struck Russia in February 2013 and it was slightly bigger than a double Decker bus, however it was travelling at forty thousand miles an hour, and it hit the Earth with thirty times more energy than the atom bomb they dropped on Hiroshima. But thankfully, due to the researchers constant monitoring they are predicting that there won't be any more collisions for at least another one hundred years. (So what are they meant to be looking for now then?)

However even if they did discover another planet heading for the earth, I don't really think they could do anything to stop the collision. Yet what I struggle to understand is why we spend all this time and vast sums of money on something we can't avoid, yet we are still quite happy to carry on needlessly destroying this planet so can you honestly say that we are not the intelligent idiots? And if you still believe I'm wrong then please explain to me why we aren't spending all that money on saving this planet from us, because you must admit there's a lot more chance of us destroying this world than any meteor.

And they are doing the same sort of thing with the search to discover how the Universe was formed and where we came from. Maybe if we spent as much time and money trying to put this planet right as we do trying to work out where the planet and we came from we wouldn't be in this mess because I really don't worry too much, about where we came from. However, I am very worried about where we are going with this planet's future, which will be a very short one indeed, unless we stop the needless destruction did you know that the smoke from the fires in the Amazon jungle are quite clearly visible from the space station.

Now I wrote this poem when I was about fourteen years old, which was very unlike me, not a bookworm this one or a poet either. Nevertheless, for some strange reason it has stuck in my mind for all these years.

Ten thousand eight hundred eons ago man was first created, ten thousand eight hundred eons have passed and man is now demented, he's mad he's crazy he's totally insane, and on this poor planet he puts all the blame. He's hacked her, and cut her and pulled her apart and generally treats her like some dirty old tart. Yet when we complain that they're raping our mother, they just smile and say oh dear, what a shame, but it don't really matter. We are destroying the earth, and this poor planet to us she gave birth, all of which I must say makes me so sad and is the proof I'm afraid that man is quite mad.

Now the intention of this book was not to insult or frighten anyone, and I sincerely hope I haven't done either. Although I do hope, it has "opened your eyes" and made you a little more aware of, and interested in, what's really happening to this world.

And hopefully realizing that the time for (peaceful) action is now before it's too late because its been predicted that mankind has a maximum of ten years to turn things around and to start returning this planet to its former glory because things are now getting out of control and it needs to stop.

We also need to dismiss the "fiction" the world governments and the big oil, gas and coal companies tell us. And we need to focus on what we know without doubt to be fact, and one of those facts is all of this, has been caused by the greediest, and the most self-centred and destructive animal on the planet, which is of course mankind. And once again I will say that I take no pleasure in saying these things about my own species and if I have upset anyone with that statement it wasn't intentional. However, I think the phrase the truth hurts will more than adequately cover that one.

So with that thought in mind I would like to thank you for your time and your support by buying this book. If you have, any comments you would like to make about this book then please feel free to email me at colinevans1954@yahoo.co.uk and I will do my utmost to answer your emails both the positive and the negative ones.

ACKNOWLEDGMENTS

I really do have to say a very big thankyou to my wife Sarah, my son Mikey, and last but by no means least my daughter Georgie for listening to me going on and on about what humanity are doing to this planet, and how someone ought to write a bloody book about it.

So, here I am, and thankyou for all your encouragement, in addition a very big thankyou to everyone mentioned in this book for realizing the potential, and taking the initiative to help, and also for getting the ball rolling.

Unfortunately, there are some I can't mention because I never received their permission to use their company names before going to print.

Of course, I must say thankyou to Sir David Attenborough for all his wildlife programmes on the television and for giving me the incentive and most of the knowledge, I needed to write this book. Also, I would like to thank my very good friends Glyn and his wife Les, in Builth Wells for being the first people to read this book and for all the encouragement to get it published.

I would also like to say thankyou to Margaret Monkman for doing the first proof reading for me, and I would like to thank Heather Takle for doing the second and final proof reading before going for publishing, so once again I thankyou all.

A BIT ABOUT MYSELF

I was born on the stroke of midnight in the front garden of my parents' house on August the 29th 1954, my place of birth was a small mining town called Bargoed in the Rhymney Valley in South Wales.

Now what my mother was doing in the garden at midnight I have absolutely no idea, (plus I was a little bit busy myself getting ready to come into this world) and sadly it will remain as one of life's little mysteries as she passed away in March 2008.

I never had much of an education as we moved around quite a bit so I pretty much taught myself to read and write, I don't know any of the times tables, and I would find it a struggle to recite the alphabet.

I left school at the age of fifteen and then got a job working in the coalmines where I stayed for about ten years. However, I have always been a bit of a wanderer (must be the Romany Gypsy blood in me) because I ended up living in a cave in Cheddar Gorge in Somerset. Then into a tent in a field at Lukey's cider farm in Shipham, then into a caravan that was owned by a friend of mine named Tom Cambridge, then I lived in a shared house in Axbridge, and eventually I got married and bought a house.

Now a writer I am not, nor a poet either, and I never thought for one minute I would be classed as either. However, I feel so strongly, about what we are doing to our home, especially when we could so easily improve it instead of needlessly destroying it for no other reason than profit that I just had to put it into words.

Lightning Source UK Ltd.
Milton Keynes UK
UKOW01f2052200218
318200UK00001B/6/P